". . . Easily the most frightening (and necessarily) the most thoroughly convincing of all modern horror stories. Its premise is that witchcraft still flourishes, an open secret among women, a closed book to men . . .

"Leiber develops this theme with the utmost dexterity, until at the story's real climax, the shocker at the end of chapter 14, I am not ashamed to say that I jumped an inch out of my seat. From that point onward, I am not really certain I touched the slipcover again until after the last page. Leiber has never written anything better."

—DAMON KNIGHT, author and critic

"High quality . . ."

—New York Times

"No one who has ever loved a witch or been witched up by one will fail to get something out of this . . ."

—Saturday Review

Also available from Ace Science Fiction,

The Fafhrd and Grey Mouser Series by Fritz Leiber:
SWORDS AGAINST DEATH
SWORDS AGAINST WIZARDRY
SWORDS AND DEVILTRY
SWORDS AND ICE MAGIC
SWORDS IN THE MIST
THE SWORDS OF LANKHMAR

Conjure Wife

FRITZ LEIBER

SF

ace books

A Division of Charter Communications Inc.
A GROSSET & DUNLAP COMPANY
51 Madison Avenue
New York, New York 10010

CONJURE WIFE

An ACE Book, by arrangement

with Twayne Publishers, Inc.

This Ace printing: July 1981

Published simultaneously in Canada

Printed in U.S.A.

CHAPTER I

NORMAN SAYLOR WAS NOT the sort of man to go prying into his wife's dressing room. That was partly the reason why he did it. He was sure that nothing could touch the security of the relationship between him and Tansy.

He knew, of course, what had happened to Bluebeard's inquisitive wife. In fact, at one time he had gone rather deeply into the psychoanalytic undertones of that strange tale of dangling ladies. But it never occurred to him that any comparable surprise might await a husband, and a modern husband at that. A half-dozen handsome beaux hanging on hooks behind that door which gleamed so creamily? The idea would have given him a chuckle in spite of his scholarly delvings into feminine psychology and those brilliant studies in the parallelisms of primitive superstition and modern neurosis that had already won him a certain professional fame.

He didn't look like a distinguished ethnologist—he was rather too young for one thing—and he certainly didn't look like a professor of sociology at Hempnell College. He quite lacked the pursed lips, frightened eyes, and tyrannical jaw of the typical faculty member of that small, proud college.

Nor did he feel at all like a good Hempnell, for which he was particularly grateful today.

Spring sunshine was streaming restfully, and the balmy air sluicing gently, through the window at his elbow. He put in the last staccato burst of typing on his long-deferred paper, "The Social Background of the Modern Voodoo Cult," and pushed himself and his chair away from his desk with a sigh of satisfaction, suddenly conscious of having reached one of those peaks in the endless cycle of happiness and unhappiness when conscience sleeps at last and everything shows its pleasant side. Such a moment as would mark for a neurotic or adolescent the beginning of a swift tumble into abysses of gloom, but which Norman had long ago learned to ride out successfully, introducing new activities at just the right time to cushion the inevitable descent.

But that didn't mean he shouldn't enjoy to the full the moment while it lasted, extract the last drop of dreamy pleasure. He wandered out of his study, flipped open a bright-backed novel, immediately deserted it to let his gaze drift past two Chinese devil-masks on the wall, ambled out past the bedroom door, smiled at the cabinet where the liquor, Hempnell-wise, was "kept in the background"—but without wanting a drink—and retraced his course as far as the bedroom.

The house was very quiet. There was something comforting this afternoon about its unpretentious size, its over-partitioned stuffiness, even its approaching senility. It seemed to wear bravely its middle-class intellectual trappings of books and prints and record-albums. Today's washable paint covered last century's ornate moldings. Overtones of intellectual freedom and love of living apologized for heavy notes of professorial dignity.

Outside the bedroom window the neighbor's boy was hauling a coaster wagon piled with newspapers. Across the street an old man was spading around some bushes, stepping gingerly over the new grass. A laundry truck rattled past, going toward the college. Norman momentarily knit his brows. Then in the opposite direction, two girl students came sauntering in the trousers and flapping shirt tails forbidden in the classrooms. Norman smiled. He was in a mood to cherish warmly the funny, cold little culture that the street represented, the narrow unamiable culture with its taboos against mentioning reality, its elaborate suppression of sex, its insistence on a stoical ability to withstand a monotonous routine of business or drudgery—and in the midst, performing the necessary rituals to keep dead ideas alive, like a college of witch-doctors in their stern stone tents, powerful, property-owning Hempnell.

It was odd, he thought, that he and Tansy had been able to stick it out so long and, in the end, so successfully. You couldn't honestly have called either of them the small-college type. Tansy especially, he was sure, had at first found everything nerve-racking: the keen-honed faculty rivalries, the lip-service to all species of respectability, the bland requirement (which would have sent a simple mechanic into spasms) that faculty wives work for the college out of pure loyalty, the elaborate social responsibilities, and the endless chaperoning of resentfully fawning students (for Hempnell was one of those colleges which offer anxious parents an alternative to the unshepherded freedom of what Norman recalled a local politician having described as ''those hotbeds of communism and free love''—the big metropolitan universities).

By all expectations Tansy and he should either have escaped to one of the hotbeds, or started a process of uneasy drifting—a squabble about academic freedom here, a question of salary there—or else tried to become writers or something equally reclusive. But somehow, drawing on an unknown inward source, Tansy had found the strength to fight Hempnell on its own terms, to conform without losing stature, to take more than her share of the social burdens and thereby draw around Norman, as it were, a magic circle, within which he had been able to carry on his real work, the researches and papers that would ultimately make them independent of Hempnell and what Hempnell thought. And not only ultimately, but soon, for now with Redding's retirement he was assured of the sociology chairmanship, and then it would only be a matter of months until one of the big universities came through with the right offer.

For a moment Norman lost himself in sudden, sharp admiration of his wife, as if he were seeing Tansy's sterling qualities for the first time. Damn it, she had done so much for him, and so unobtrusively. Even to acting as a tireless and efficient secretary on all his researches without once making him feel guilty in his gratefulness. And he had been such unpromising material to start with: a lazy, spottily brilliant young instructor, dangerously contemptuous of academic life, taking a sophomoric pleasure in shocking his staid colleagues, with a suicidal tendency to make major issues out of minor disputes with deans and presidents. Why, there had been a dozen times during the early years when he had teetered on the brink of the academic downgrade, when there had loomed some irreparable break with authority, yet he had always managed to wriggle out, and almost always, he could see, looking back, with Tansy's clever, roundabout aid. Ever since he had married her, his life had been luck, luck, luck!

How the devil had she managed it?—she, who had been as lazy and wantonly rebellious as himself, a moody, irresponsible girl, daughter of an ineffectual country minister, her childhood lonely and undisciplined, solaced by wild imaginings, with little or nothing of the routinized, middle-class stuffiness that helped so much at Hempnell.

Nevertheless she had managed it, so that now—what a paradox!—he was looked upon as "a good, solid Hempnell man," "a credit to the college," "doing big things," close friend to Dean Gunnison (who wasn't such a terrible sort himself when you got to know him) and a man on whom platitudinous President Pollard "depended," a tower of strength compared to his nervous, rabbit-brained department colleague Hervey Sawtelle. From being one of the iconoclasts, he had become one of the plaster images, and yet (and this was the really wonderful thing) without once compromising his serious ideals, without once knuckling under to reactionary rulings.

Now, in his reflective, sun-brightened mood, it seemed to Norman that there was something incredible about his success at Hempnell, something magical and frightening, as if he and Tansy were a young warrior and squaw who had blundered into a realm of ancestral ghosts and had managed to convince those grim phantoms that they too were properly buried tribal elders, fit to share the supernatural rulership; always managing to keep secret their true flesh-and-blood nature despite a thousand threatened disclosures, because Tansy happened to know the right protective charms. Of course, when you came down to it, it was just that they were both mature and realistic. Everybody had to get over that age-old hump, learn to control the childish ego or else have his life wrecked by it. Still . . .

The sunlight brightened a trifle, became a shade more golden, as if some cosmic electrician had advanced the switch another notch. At the same moment one of the two shirt-tailed girls, disappearing around the corner of the house next door, laughed happily. Norman turned back from the window and as he did, Totem the cat rose from her sun-warmed spot on the silk comforter and indulged in a titanic yawn-and-stretch that looked as if it surely would dislocate every bone in her handsome body. Grateful for the example, Norman copied her, in moderation. Oh, it was a wonderful day all right, one of those days when reality becomes a succession of such bright and sharp images that you are afraid that any moment you will poke a hole in the gorgeous screen and glimpse the illimitable, unknown blackness it films; when everything seems so friendly and right that you tremble lest a sudden searing flash of insight reveal to you the massed horror and hate and brutality and ignorance of which life rests.

As Norman finished his yawn, he became aware that his blissful mood had still a few moments to run.

At the same instant his gaze happened to swing to the door of Tansy's dressing room.

He was conscious of wanting to do one more thing before he buckled down to work or recreation, something completely idle and aimless, a shade out of character, perhaps even a little childish and reprehensible, so he could be amusedly ashamed afterwards.

Of course, if Tansy had been there . . . but since she wasn't, her dressing room might serve as a proxy of her amiable self.

The door stood enticingly ajar, revealing the edge of a fragile chair with a discarded slip trailing down from it and a feathery-toed mule peeking from under. Beyond the chair was a jar-strewn section of ivory table-top, pleasantly dusky—for it was a windowless small cubicle, hardly more than a large closet.

He had never in his life spied on Tansy or seriously thought of doing so, any more than, so far as he knew, she had on him. It was one of those things they had taken for granted as a fundamental of marriage.

But this thing he was tempted toward couldn't be called spying. It was more like a gesture of illicit love, in any case a trifling transgression.

Besides, no human being has the right to consider himself perfect, or even completely adult, to bottle up all naughty urges.

Moreover, he had carried away from the sunny window a certain preoccupation with the riddle of Tansy, the secret of her ability to withstand and best the strangling atmosphere of catclawed Hempnell. Hardly a riddle, of course, and certainly not one to which you could hope to find the answer in her boudoir. Still . . .

He hesitated.

Totem, her white paws curled neatly under her black waistcoat, watched him.

He walked into Tansy's dressing room.

Totem sprang down from the bed and padded after him.

He switched on the rose-shaded lamp and surveyed the rack of dresses, the shelves of shoes. There was a slight disorder, very sane and lovable. A faint perfume conjured up agreeable memories.

He studied the photographs on the wall around the mirror.

One of Tansy and himself in partial Indian costume, from three summers back when he had been studying the Yumas. They both looked solemn, as if trying very seriously to be good Indians. Another, rather faded, showed them in 1928 bathing suits, standing on an old pier smiling squintily with the sun in their eyes. That took him back east to Bayport, the summer before they were married. A third showed an uproarious Negro baptism in midriver. That was when he had held the Hazelton Fellowship and been gathering materials for his *Social Patterns of the Southern Negro* and later "Feminine Element in Superstition." Tansy had been invaluable to him that busy half-year when he had hammered out the groundwork of a reputation. She had accompanied him in the field, writing down the vivid, rambling recollections of ancient, bright-eyed men and women who remembered the slave days because they themselves had been slaves. He recalled how slight and boyish and intense she'd seemed, even a little gauche, that summer when they'd just left Gorham College before coming to Hempnell. She'd certainly gained remarkably in poise since then.

The fourth picture showed an old Negro conjure doctor with wrinkled face and proud high forehead under a battered slouch hat. He stood with shoulders back and eyes quietly flaring, as if surveying the whole dirty-pink culture and rejecting it because he had a deeper and stronger knowledge of his own. Ostrich plumes and scarified cheeks couldn't have made him look any more impressive. Norman remembered the fellow well—he had been one of their more valuable and also more difficult informants, requiring several visits before the notebook had been satisfied.

He looked down at the dressing table and the ample array of cosmetics. Tansy had been the first of the Hempnell faculty wives to use lipstick and lacquer her nails. There had been veiled criticism and some talk of "the example we set our students," but she had stuck it out until Hulda Gunnison had appeared at the Faculty Frolic with a careless but unmistakable crimson smear on her mouth. Then all had been well.

Flanked by cold cream jars was a small photograph of

himself, with a little pile of small change, all dimes and quarters, in front of it.

He roused himself. This wasn't the vaguely illegitimate spying he had intended. He pulled out a drawer at random, hastily scanned the pile of rolled-up stockings that filled it, shut it, took hold of the ivory knob of the next.

And paused.

This was rather silly, it occurred to him. Simultaneously he realized that he had just squeezed the last drop from the peak of his mood. As when he had turned from the window, but more ominously, the moment seemed to freeze, as if all reality, every bit of it he lived to this moment, were something revealed by a lightning flash that would the next instant blink out, leaving inky darkness. That rather common buzzing-in-the-ears, everything-too-real sensation.

From the doorway Totem looked up at him.

But sillier still to analyze a trifling whim, as if it could mean anything one way or the other.

To show it didn't, he'd look in one more drawer.

It jammed, so he gave it a sharp tug before it jerked free.

A large cardboard box toward the back caught his eye. He edged up the cover and took out one of the tiny glass-stoppered bottles that filled it. What sort of a cosmetic would this be? Too dark for face powder. More like a geologist's soil specimen. An ingredient for a mud pack? Hardly. Tansy had a herb garden. Could that be involved?

The dry, dark-brown granules shifted smoothly, like sand in an hourglass, as he rotated the glass cylinder. The label appeared, in Tansy's clear script. ''Julia Trock, Roseland.'' He couldn't recall any Julia Trock. And why should the name Roseland seem distasteful? His hand knocked aside the cardboard cover as he reached for a second bottle, identical with the first, except that the contents had a somewhat reddish tinge and the label read, ''Phillip Lassiter, Hill.'' A third, contents same color as the first: ''J. P. Thorndyke, Roseland.'' Then a handful, quickly snatched up: ''Emelyn Scatterday, Roseland.'' ''Mortimer Pope, Hill.'' ''The Rev.

Bufort Ames, Roseland.'' They were, respectively, brown, reddish, and brown.

The silence in the house grew thunderous; even the sunlight in the bedroom seemed to sizzle and fry, as his mind rose to a sudden pitch of concentration on the puzzle. ''Roseland and Hill, Roseland and Hill, Oh we went to Roseland and Hill,''—like a nursery rhyme somehow turned nasty, making the glass cylinders repugnant to his fingers, ''—but we never came back.''

Abruptly the answer came.

The two local cemeteries.

Graveyard dirt.

Soil specimens all right. Graveyard dirt from particular graves. A chief ingredient of Negro conjure magic.

With a soft thud Totem landed on the table and began to sniff inquisitively at the bottles, springing away as Norman plunged his hand into the drawer. He felt smaller boxes behind the big one, yanked suddenly at the whole drawer, so it fell to the floor. In one of the boxes were bent, rusty, worn bits of iron—horseshoe nails. In the other were calling-card envelopes, filled with snippings of hair, each labeled like the bottles. But he knew most of those names—''Hervey Sawtelle . . . Gracine Pollard . . . Hulda Gunnison . . .'' And in one labeled ''Evelyn Sawtelle''—red-lacquered nail clippings.

In the third drawer he drew blank. But the fourth yielded a varied harvest. Packets of small dried leaves and powdered vegetable matter—so that was what came from Tansy's herb garden along with kitchen seasonings? Vervain, vinmoin, devil's stuff, the labels said. Bits of lodestone with iron fillings clinging to them. Goose quills which spilled quicksilver when he shook them. Small squares of flannel, the sort that Negro conjure doctors use for their ''tricken bags'' or ''hands.'' A box of old silver coins and silver filings—strong protective magic; giving significance to the silver coins in front of his photograph.

But Tansy was so sane, so healthily contemptuous of

palmistry, astrology, numerology and all other superstitious fads. A hardheaded New Englander. So well versed, from her work with him, in the psychological background of superstition and primitive magic. So well versed—

He found himself thumbing through a dog-eared copy of his own *Parallelisms in Superstition and Neurosis*. It looked like the one he had lost around the house—was it eight years ago? Beside a formula for conjuration was a marginal notation in Tansy's script: "Doesn't work. Substitute copper filings for brass. Try in dark of moon instead of full."

"Norman—"

Tansy was standing in the doorway.

CHAPTER II

It is the people we know best who can, on rare occasions, seem most unreal to us. For a moment the familiar face registers as merely an arbitrary arrangement of colored surfaces, without even the shadowy personality with which we invest a strange face glimpsed in the street.

Norman Saylor felt he wasn't looking at his wife, but at a painting of her. It was as if some wizardly Renoir or Toulouse-Lautrec had painted Tansy with the air for a canvas—boldly blocked in the flat cheeks in pale flesh tones faintly under-tinged with green, drew them together to a small defiant chin; smudged crosswise with careless art the red thoughtful lips, the gray-green maybe humorous eyes, the narrow low-arched brows with single vertical furrow between; created with one black stroke the childishly sinister bangs, swiftly smeared the areas of shadowed white throat and wine-colored dress; caught perfectly the feel of the elbow that hugged a package from the dressmaker's, as the small ugly hands lifted to remove a tiny hat that was another patch of the wine color with a highlight representing a little doodad of silvered glass.

If he were to reach out and touch her, Norman felt, the

paint would peel down in strips from the empty air, as from some walking sister-picture of Dorian Gray.

He stood stupidly staring at her, the open book in his hand. He didn't hear himself say anything, though he knew that if words had come to his lips at that moment, his voice would have sounded to him like another's—some fool professor's.

Then, without saying anything either, and without any noticeable change of expression, Tansy turned on her heel and walked rapidly out of the bedroom. The package from the dressmaker's fell to the floor. It was a moment before Norman could stir himself.

He caught up with her in the living room. She was headed for the front door. When he realized she wasn't going to turn or stop, he threw his arms around her. And then, at last, she did react. She struggled like an animal, but with her face turned sharply away and her arms flat against her sides, as if tied there.

Through taut mouth-slit, in a very low voice, but spitting-ly, she said, "Don't touch me."

Norman strained and braced his feet. There was something horrible about the way she threw herself from side to side, trying to break his embrace. There flickered in his mind the thought of a woman in a straitjacket.

She kept repeating "Don't touch me" in the same tones, and he kept imploring, "But Tansy—"

Suddenly she stopped struggling. He dropped his arms and stepped back.

She didn't relax. She just stood there rigidly, her face twisted to one side—and from what he could see of it, the eyes were winced shut and the lips bitten together. Some kindred tightness, inside him, hurt his heart.

"Darling!" he said. "I'm ashamed of what I did. No matter what it led to, it was a cheap, underhanded unworthy action. But—"

"It's not that!"

He hesitated. "You mean, you're acting this way because you're, well, ashamed of what I found out?"

No reply.

"Please, Tansy, we've got to talk about it."

Still no reply. He unhappily fingered the air. "But I'm sure everything will be all right. If you'll just tell me . . .

"Tansy, please . . ."

Her posture didn't alter, but her lips arched and the words were spat out: "Why don't you strap me and stick pins in me? They used to do that."

"Darling, I'd do anything rather than hurt you! But this is something that just has to be talked about."

"I can't. If you say another word about it, I'll scream!"

"Darling, if I possibly could, I'd stop. But this is one of those things. We've just got to talk it over."

"I'd rather die."

"But you've got to tell me. You've got to!"

He was shouting.

For a moment he thought she was going to faint. He reached forward to catch her. But it was only that her body had abruptly gone slack. She walked over to the nearest chair, dropped her hat on a small table beside, sat down listlessly.

"All right," she said. "Let's talk about it."

6:37 P.M.: The last rays of sunlight sliced the bookcase, touched the red teeth of the left-hand devil mask. Tansy was sitting on one end of the davenport, while Norman was at the other, turned sideways with one knee on the cushion, watching her.

Tansy switched around, flirting her head irritably, as if there were in the air a smoke of words which had grown unendurably thick. "All right, have it your own way then! I was very seriously trying to use conjure magic. I was doing everything a civilized woman shouldn't. I was trying to put spells on people and things. I was trying to change the future. I was . . . oh, the whole works!"

Norman gave a small jerky nod. It was the same sort of nod he gave at student conferences, when after seeming hours of muddled discussion, some blank-faced young hopeful would begin to get a glimmering of what they were really talking about. He leaned toward her.

"But why?"

"To protect you and your career." She was looking at her lap.

"But knowing all you did about the background of superstition, how did you ever come to believe—?" His voice wasn't loud now. It was cool, almost a lawyer's.

She twisted. "I don't know. When you put it that way . . . of course. But when you desperately want things to happen, or not to happen, to someone you love . . . I was only doing what millions of others have done. And then, you see, Norm, the things I did . . . well, they seemed to work . . . at least most of the time."

"But don't you see," he continued smoothly, "that those very exceptions prove that the things you were doing *didn't* work? That the successes were just coincidences?"

Her voice rose a trifle. "I don't know about that. There might have been counter-influences at work—" She turned toward him impulsively. "Oh, I don't know what I believe! I've never really been sure that my charms worked. There was no way of telling. Don't you see, once I'd started, I didn't dare stop?"

"And you've been doing it all these years?"

She nodded unhappily. "Ever since we came to Hempnell."

He looked at her, trying to comprehend it. It was almost impossible to take at one gulp the realization that in the mind of this trim modern creature he had known in completest intimacy, there was a whole great area he had never dreamed of, an area that was part and parcel of the dead practices he analyzed in books, an area that belonged to the Stone Age and never to him, an area plunged in darkness, acrouch with fear, blown by giant winds. He tried to picture Tansy muttering charms, stitching up flannel hands by candlelight, visiting graveyards and God knows what other places in search of ingredients. His imagination almost failed. And yet it had all been happening right under his nose.

The only faintly suspicious aspect of Tansy's behavior that he could recall was her whim for taking "little walks" by herself. If he had ever wondered about Tansy and superstitions at all, it had only been to decide, with a touch of self-congratulation, that for a woman she was almost oddly free from irrationality.

"Oh, Norm, I'm so confused and miserable," she broke in. "I don't know what to say or how to start."

He had an answer for that, a scholar's answer.

"Tell me how it all happened, right from the beginning."

7:54: They were still sitting on the davenport. The room was almost dark. The devil masks were irregular ovals of gloom. Tansy's face was a pale smudge. Norman couldn't study its expression, but judging from her voice, it had become animated.

"Hold on a minute," he interrupted. "Let's get some things straight. You say you were very much afraid when we first came to Hempnell to arrange about my job, before I went south on the Hazelton Fellowship?"

"Oh, yes, Norm. Hempnell terrified me. Everyone was so obviously antagonistic and so deadly respectable. I knew I'd be a flop as a professor's wife—I was practically told so to my face. I don't know which was worse. Hulda Gunnison looking me up and down and grunting contemptuously, 'I guess you'll do,' when I made the mistake of confiding in her, or old Mrs. Carr petting my arm and saying, 'I know you and your husband will be very happy here at Hempnell. You're young, but Hempnell loves nice young folk!' Against those women I felt completely unprotected. And your career too."

"Right. So when I took you south and plunged you into the midst of the most superstition-swayed area in the whole country, exposed you to the stuff night and day, you were ripe for its promise of magical security."

Tansy laughed half-heartedly. "I don't know about the ripe part, but it certainly impressed me. I drank in all I could. At the back of my mind, I suppose, was the feeling: Some day I may need this. And when we went back to Hempnell in the fall, I felt more confident."

Norman nodded. That fitted. Come to think of it, there had

been something unnatural about the intense, silent en-
thusiasm with which Tansy had plunged into boring secreta-
rial work right after their marriage.

"But you didn't actually try and conjure magic," he
continued, "until I got pneumonia that first winter?"

"That's right. Until then, it was just a cloud of vaguely
reassuring ideas—scraps of things I'd find myself saying
over when I woke in the middle of the night, things I'd
unconsciously avoid doing because they were unlucky, like
sweeping the steps after dark or crossing knives and forks.
And then when you got pneumonia, well, when the person
you love is near death, you'll try anything."

For a moment Norman's voice was sympathetic. "Of
course." Then the classroom tone came back. "But I gather
that it wasn't until I had that brush with Pollard over sex
education and came off decently, and especially until my
book came out in 1931 and got such, well, pretty favorable
reviews, that you really began to believe that your magic was
working?"

"That's right."

Norman sat back. "Oh, Lord," he said.

"What's the matter, dear? You don't feel I'm trying to
take any credit away from you for the book's success?"

Norman half laughed, half snorted. "Good Lord, no.
But—" He stopped himself. "Well, that takes us to 1930.
Go on from there."

8:58: Norman reached over and switched on the light,
winced at its glare. Tansy ducked her head.

He stood up, massaging the back of his neck.

"The things that gets me," he said, "is the way it invaded
every nook and corner of your life, bit by bit, so that finally
you couldn't take a step, or rather let me take one, without there having to be some protective charm. It's almost
like—"

He was going to say, "Some kinds of paranoia."

Tansy's voice was hoarse and whispery. "I even wear
hooks-and-eyes instead of zippers because the hooks are
supposed to catch evil spirits. And the mirror-decorations on

my hats and bags and dresses—you've guessed it, they're Tibetan magic to reflect away misfortune.''

He stood in front of her. ''Look, Tansy, whatever made you do it?''

''I've just told you.''

''I know, but what made you stick to it year after year, when as you've admitted, you always suspected you were just fooling yourself? I could understand it with another woman, but with you . . . .''

Tansy hesitated. ''I know you'll think I'm being romantic and trite, but I've always felt that women were more primitive than men, closer to ancient feelings.'' She hurried over that. ''And then there were things I remembered from childhood. Queer mistaken ideas I got from my father's sermons. Stories one of the old ladies there used to tell us. Hints.'' (Norman thought: Country parsonage! Healthy mental atmosphere, not!) ''And then—oh, there were a thousand other things. But I'll try to tell them to you.''

''Swell,'' he said, putting his hand on her shoulder. ''But we'd better eat something along with it.''

9:17: They were sitting facing each other in the jolly red-and-white kitchen. On the table were untasted sandwiches and half-sipped cups of black coffee. It was obvious that the situation between them had changed. Now it was Norman who looked away and Tansy who studied expressions anxiously.

''Well, Norman,'' she managed to say finally, ''do you think I'm crazy, or going crazy?''

It was just the question he had needed. ''No, I don't,'' he said levelly. ''Though Lord only knows what an outsider would think if he found out what you'd been doing. But just as surely as you aren't crazy, you are neurotic—like all of us—and your neurosis has taken a darned unusual form.''

Suddenly aware of hunger, he picked up a sandwich and began to munch it as he talked, nibbling the edge all around and then beginning to work in.

''Look, all of us have private rituals—our own little peculiar ways of eating and drinking and sleeping and going to the bathroom. Rituals we're hardly conscious of, but that would look mighty strange if analyzed. You know, to step or not to step on cracks in the sidewalk. Things like that. Now I'd say that your private rituals, because of the special circumstances of your life, have gotten all tangled up with conjure magic, so you can hardly tell which is which." He paused. "Now here's an important thing. So long as only *you* knew what you were doing, you didn't tend to criticize your entanglement with conjure magic any more than the average person criticizes his magic formula for going to sleep. There was no social conflict."

He started to pace, still eating the sandwich.

"Good Lord, haven't I devoted a good part of my life to investigating how and why men and women are superstiti- And shouldn't I have been aware of the contagious effect of that study on you? And what is superstition, but misguided, unobjective science? And when it comes down to that, is it to be wondered if people grasp at superstition in this rotten, hate-filled, half-doomed world of today? Lord knows, I'd welcome the blackest of black magic, if it could do anything to stave off the atom bomb."

Tansy had risen. Her eyes looked unnaturally large and bright.

"Then," she faltered, "you honestly don't hate me, or think I'm going crazy?"

He put his arms around her. "Hell no!"

She began to cry.

9:33: They were sitting on the davenport again. Tansy had stopped crying, but her head still rested against his shoulder.

For a while they were quiet. Then Norman spoke. He used the deceptively mild tones of a doctor telling a patient that another operation will be necessary.

"Of course, you'll have to quit doing it now."

Tansy sat up quickly. "Oh, no, Norm, I couldn't."

"Why not? You've just agreed it was all nonsense. You've just thanked me for opening your eyes."

"I know that, but still—don't make me, Norm!"

"Now be reasonable, Tansy," he said. "You've taken

this like a major so far. I'm proud of you. But don't you see, you can't stop half way. Once you've started to face this weakness of yours logically, you've got to keep on. You've got to get rid of all that stuff in your dressing room, all the charms you've hidden around, everything.''

She shook her head. ''Don't make me, Norm,'' she repeated. ''Not all at once. I'd feel naked.''

''No you won't. You'll feel stronger. Because you'll find out that what you half thought might be magic, is really your own unaided ability.''

''No, Norm. Why do I have to stop? What difference does it make? You said yourself it was just nonsense—a private ritual.''

''But now that I know about it, it's not private any more. And in any case,'' he added, almost dangerously, ''it's a pretty unusual ritual.''

''But couldn't I just quit by degrees?'' She pleaded, like a child. ''You know, not lay any new charms, but leave the old ones?''

He shook his head. ''No,'' he said, ''it's like giving up drink—it has to be a clean break.''

Her voice began to rise. ''But, Norm, I can't do it. I simply can't!''

He began to feel she was a child. ''Tansy, you must.''

''But there wasn't ever anything bad about my magic.'' The childishness was getting frightening. ''I never used it to hurt anyone or to ask for unreasonable things, like making you president of Hempnell overnight. I only wanted to protect you.''

''Tansy, what difference does that make!''

Her breasts were heaving. ''I tell you, Norm, I won't be responsible for what happens to you if you make me take away those protections.''

''Tansy, be reasonable. What on earth do I need with protections of that sort?''

''Oh, so you think that everything you've won in life is just the result of your own unaided abilities? You don't recognize the luck in it?''

Norman remembered thinking the same thing himself this afternoon and that made him angrier. "Now Tansy—"

"And you think that everyone loves you and wishes you well, don't you? You think all those beasts over at Hempnell are just a lot of pussies with their claws clipped? You pass off their spite and jealousies as something trivial, beneath your notice. Well, let me tell you—"

"Tansy, stop screaming!"

"—that there are those at Hempnell who would like to see you dead—and who would have seen you dead a long time ago, if they could have worked it!"

"Tansy!"

"What do you suppose Evelyn Sawtelle feels toward you for the way you're nosing out her flutterbudget of a husband for the sociology chairmanship? Do you think she wants to bake you a cake? One of her cherry-chocolate ones? How do you suppose Hulda Gunnison likes the influence you have acquired over her husband? It's mainly because of you that she no longer runs the Dean of Men's office. And as for that libidinous old bitch Mrs. Carr, do you imagine that she enjoys the way your freedom-and-frankness policy with the students is cutting into her holier-than-thou respectability, her 'Sex is just an ugly word' stuff? What do you think those women have been doing for *their* husbands?"

"Oh, Lord, Tansy, why drag in that old faculty jealousies business?"

"Do you suppose they'd stop at mere protection? Do you imagine women like that would observe any distinction between white magic and black?"

"Tansy! You don't know what you're saying. If you mean to imply—Tansy, when you talk that way, you actually sound like a witch."

"Oh, I do?" For a moment her expression was so tight her face looked all skull. "Well, maybe I am. And maybe it's lucky for you I've been one."

He grabbed her by the arm. "Listen, I've been patient with you about all this ignorant nonsense. But now you're going to show some sense and show it quick."

Her lips curled, nastily. "Oh, I see. It's been the velvet glove so far, but now it's going to be the iron hand. If I don't do just as you say, I get packed off to an asylum. Is that it?"

"Of course not! But you've just got to be sensible."

"Well, I tell you I won't!"

"Now, Tansy—"

10:13: The folded comforter jounced as Tansy flopped on the bed. New tears had streaked and reddened her face and dried. "All right," she said, in a stuffy voice. "I'll do what you want. I'll burn all my things."

Norman felt light-headed. The thought came into his mind, "And to think I dared to tackle it without a psychiatrist!"

"There've been enough times when I've wanted to stop," she added. "Just like there've been times I've wanted to stop being a woman."

What followed struck Norman as weirdly anticlimactic. First the ransacking of Tansy's dressing room for hidden charms and paraphernalia. Norman found himself remembering those old two-reel comedies in which scores of people pile out of a taxicab—it seemed impossible that a few shallow drawers and old shoe boxes could hold so many wastepaper baskets of junk. He tossed the dog-eared copy of "Parallelisms" on top of the last one, picked up Tansy's leather-bound diary. She shook her head reassuringly. After the barest hesitation he put it back unopened.

Then the rest of the house. Tansy moving faster and faster, darting from room to room, deftly recovering flannel-wrapped "hands" from the upholstery of the chair, the under sides of table tops, the interior of vases, until Norman dizzily marveled that he had lived in the house for more than ten years without chancing on any.

"It's rather like a treasure hunt, isn't it?" she said with a rueful smile.

There were other charms outside—under front and back doorsteps, in the garage, and in the car. With every handful thrown on the roaring fire he had built in the living room, Norman's sense of relief grew. Finally Tansy opened the seams of the pillows on his bed and carefully fished out two little matted shapes made of feathers bound with fine thread so that they had blended with the fluffy contents of the pillow.

"See, one's a heart, the other an anchor. That's for security," she told him. "New Orleans feather magic. You haven't taken a step for years without being in the range of one of my protective charms."

The feather figures puffed into flame.

"There," she said. "Feel any reaction?"

"No," he said. "Any reason I should?"

She shook her head. "Except that those were the last ones. And so, if there *were* any hostile forces that my charms were keeping at bay . . ."

He laughed tolerantly. Then for a moment his voice grew hard. "You're sure they're all gone? Absolutely certain you haven't overlooked any?"

"Absolutely certain. There's not one left in the house or near it, Norm—and I never planted any anywhere else because I was afraid of . . . well, interference. I've counted them all over in my mind a dozen times and they've all gone—" She looked at the fire, "—pouf. And now," she said quietly, "I'm tired, really tired. I want to go straight to bed."

Suddenly she began to laugh. "Oh, but first I'll have to stitch up those pillows, or else there'll be feathers all over the place."

He put his arms around her. "Everything okay now?"

"Yes, darling. There's only one thing I want to ask you—that we don't talk about this for a few days at least. Not even mention it. I don't think I could . . . . Will you promise me that, Norm?"

He pulled her closer. "Absolutely dear, Absolutely."

CHAPTER III

LEANING FORWARD FROM THE WORN leather edge of the old easy chair, Norman played with the remnants of the fire, tapped the fang of the poker against a glowing board until it collapsed into tinkling embers, over which swayed almost invisible blue flames.

From the floor beside him Totem watched the flames, head between outstretched paws.

Norman felt tired. He really ought to have followed Tansy to bed long ago, except he wanted time for his thoughts to unkink. Rather a bother, this professional need to assimilate each new situation, to pick over its details mentally, turning them this way and that, until they became quite shopworn. Whereas Tansy had turned out her thoughts like a light and plunged into sleep. How like Tansy!—or perhaps it was just the more finely attuned, hyperthyroid female physiology.

In any case, she'd done the practical, sensible thing. And that was like Tansy, too. Always fair. Always willing, in the long run, to listen to logic (in a similar situation would he have dared try reasoned argument on any other woman?). Always . . . yes . . . empirical. Except that she had gotten off on a crazy sidetrack.

Hempnell was responsible for that, it was a breeding place for neurosis, and being a faculty wife put a woman in one of the worst spots. He ought to have realized years ago the strain she was under and taken steps. But she'd been too good an actor for him. And he was always forgetting just how deadly seriously women took faculty intrigues. They couldn't escape like their husbands into the cool, measured worlds of mathematics, microbiology or what have you.

Norman smiled. That had been an odd notion Tansy had let slip toward the end—that Evelyn Sawtelle and Harold Gunnison's wife and old Mrs. Carr were practicing magic too, of the venomous black variety. And not any too hard to believe, either, if you knew them! That was the sort of idea with which a clever satirical writer could do a lot. Just carry it a step further—picture most women as glamor-conscious witches, carrying on their savage warfare of deathspell and countercharm, while their reality-befuddled husbands went blithely about their business. Let's see, Barrie had written *What Every Woman Knows* to show that men never realize how their wives were responsible for their successes. Being that blind, would men be any more apt to realize that their wives used witchcraft for the purpose?

Norm's smile changed to a wince. He had just remembered that it wasn't just an odd notion, but that Tansy had actually believed, or half-believed, such things. He sucked his lips wryly. Doubtless he'd have more unpleasant moments like this, when memory would catch him up with a start. After tonight, it was inevitable.

Still, the worst was over.

He reached down to stroke Totem, who did not look away from the hypnotic embers.

"Time we got to bed, old cat. Must be about twelve. No—quarter past one."

As he slipped the watch back into his pocket, the fingers of his left hand went to the locket at the other end of the chain.

He weighted in his palm the small golden heart, a gift from Tansy. Was it perhaps a trifle heavier than its metal shell could account for? He snapped up the cover with his thumbnail. There was no regular way of getting at the space behind Tansy's picture, so after a moment's hesitation, he carefully edged out the tiny photograph with a pencil point.

Behind the photograph was a tiny packet wrapped in the finest flannel.

Just like a woman—that thought came with vicious swiftness—to seem to give in completely, but to hold out on something.

Perhaps she had forgotten.

Angrily he tossed the packet into the fireplace. The photograph fluttered along with it, lighted on the bed of embers, and flared before he could snatch it out. He had a glimpse of Tansy's face curling and blackening.

The packet took longer. A yellow glow crept across its surface, as the nap singed. Then a wavering four-inch flame shot up.

Simultaneously a chill went through him, though he still felt the heat from the embers. The room seemed to darken. There was a faint, mighty roaring in his ears, as of motors far underground. He had the sense of standing suddenly naked and unarmed before something menacingly alien.

Totem had turned around and was peering intently at the shadows in the far corner. With a spitting hiss she sprang sideways and darted from the room.

Norman realized he was trembling. Nervous reaction, he told himself. Might have known it was overdue.

The flame died, and once again there was only the frostily tinkling bed of embers.

Explosively, the phone began to jangle.

"Professor Saylor? I don't suppose you ever thought you'd hear from me again, did you? Well, the reason I'm calling you is that I always believe in letting people—no matter who—know where I stand, which is a lot more than can be said for some people."

Norman held the receiver away from his ear. The words, though jumbled, sounded like the beginning of a call, but the tone in which they were uttered didn't. Surely it would take half an hour of ranting before anyone could reach such a pitch of whining and—yes, the word was applicable—insane anger.

"What I want to tell you, Saylor, is this: I'm not going to take what's been done to my lying down. I'm not going to let myself stay flunked out of Hempnell. I'm going to demand to have my grades changed and you know why!"

Norman recognized the voice. There sprang into his mind the image of a pale, abnormally narrow face with pouting lips and protuberant eyes, crowned by a great shock of red hair. He cut in.

"Now listen, Jennings, if you thought you were being treated unfairly, why didn't you present your grievances two months ago, when you got your grades?"

"Why? Because I let you pull the wool over my eyes. The open-minded Professor Saylor! It wasn't until afterwards that I realized how you hadn't given me the proper attention, how I'd been slighted or bamboozled at conferences, how you didn't tell me I might flunk until it was too late, how you based your tests on trick questions from lectures I'd missed, how you discriminated against me because of my father's politics and because I wasn't the student type like that Bronstein. It wasn't until then—"

"Jennings, be reasonable. You flunked two courses besides mine last semester."

"Yes, because you passed the word around, influenced others against me, made them see me as you pretended to see me, made everyone—"

"And you mean to tell me you only now realized all this?"

"Yes I do. It just came to me in a flash as I was thinking here. Oh, you were clever, all right. You had me eating out of your hand, you had me taking everything lying down, you had me scared. But once I got my first suspicion, I saw the whole plot clear as day. Everything fitted, everything led back to you, everything—"

"Including the fact that you were flunked out of two other colleges before you ever came to Hempnell?"

"There! I knew you were prejudiced against me from the start!"

"Jennings," Norman said wearily, "I've listened to all I'm going to. If you have any grievances, present them to Dean Gunnison."

"Do you mean to say you won't take any action?"

"Yes, I mean just that."

"Is that final?"

"Yes, it's final."

"Very well, Saylor. Then all I can say to you is, watch out! Watch out, Saylor! Watch out!"

There was a click at the other end of the line. Norman gently put the phone back in its cradle. Oh, damn Theodore Jennings' parents! Not because they were hypocritical, vain, reactionary stuffed-shirts, but because they had such cruel pride that they were determined to shove through college a sensitive, selfish, wordy, somewhat subnormal boy, as narrow-minded as they were though not one-tenth as canny. And damn President Pollard for kow-towing so ineptly to their wealth and political influence that he had let the boy into Hempnell knowing perfectly well he'd fail.

Norman put the screen in front of the fire, switched out the living room lights and started toward the bedroom in the yellow glow fanning out from the hall.

Again the phone jangled. Norman looked at it curiously for a moment before he picked it up.

"Hello."

There was no reply. He waited for a few moments. Then, "Hello?" he repeated.

Still there was no reply. He was about to hang up when he thought he caught the sound of breathing—excited, uneven, choked.

"Who is it?" he said sharply. "This is Professor Saylor. Please speak up."

He still seemed to hear the breathing. That was all.

Then out of the small black mystery of the phone came out word, enunciated slowly and with difficulty, in a voice that was deep yet throbbed with an almost fantastic intimacy.

"Darling!"

Norman swallowed. He didn't seem to recognize this voice at all. Before he could think what to say, it went on, more swiftly, but otherwise unchanged.

"Oh, Norman, how glad I am that at last I've found the courage to speak where you wouldn't. I'm ready now, darling, I'm ready. You only need to come to me."

"Really?" Norman temporized in amazement. It seemed to him now that there was something faintly familiar about the voice, not in its tone, but in its phrasing and rhythm.

"Come to me, lover, come to me. Take me to some place where we'll be alone. All alone. I'll be your mistress. I'll be your slave. Subject me to you. Do anything you want to me."

Norman wanted to laugh uproariously, yet his heart was pounding a little. Nice, perhaps, if it were real, but there was something so clownish about it. Was it a joke? he suddenly asked himself.

"I'm lying here talking to you without any clothes on, darling. There's just a tiny pink lamp by the bed. Oh, take me to some lonely tropical isle and we'll make passionate love together. I'll hurt you and you'll hurt me. And then we'll swim in the moonlight with white petals drifting down onto the water."

Yes, it was a joke all right, it just had to be, he decided with a twinge of only half-humorous regret. And then there suddenly occurred to him the one person capable of playing such a joke.

"So come, Norman, come, and take me into the darkness," the voice continued.

"All right, I will," he replied briskly. "And after I've made passionate love to you I'll switch on the lights and I'll say, 'Mona Utell, aren't you ashamed of yourself?' "

"Mona?" The voice rose in pitch. "Mona?"

"Yes indeed, Mona!" he assured her laughingly. "You're the only actress I know, in fact the only woman I know, who could do that corny sultriness to such perfection.

What would have have done if Tansy had answered? An imitation of Humphrey Bogart? How's New York? How's the party? What are you drinking?''

"Drinking? Norman, don't you know who this is?''

"Certainly. You're Mona Utell.'' But he had already grown doubtful. Long-drawn-out jokes weren't Mona's specialty. And the strange voice, with its aura of exasperating familiarity, was growing higher all the time.

"You really don't know who I am?''

"No, I guess I don't,'' he replied, speaking a little sharply because that was the way the question had been put.

"Not really?''

Norman sensed that those two words cocked the trigger for an emotional explosion, but he didn't care. He went ahead and pulled it. "No!'' he said impatiently.

At that the voice at the other end of the wire rose to a scream. Totem, slinking past, turned her head at the sound.

"You beast! You dirty beast! After all you've done to me! After you've deliberately roused me. After you've undressed me a hundred times with your eyes!''

"Now please—''

"Corny sultriness! You . . . you lousy schoolteacher! Go back to your Mona! Go back to that snippy wife of yours. And I hope you all three fry in hell!''

Once again Norman found himself listening to a dead phone. With a wry smile he put it down. Oh, the staid life of a college professor! He tried to think of some woman who could possibly be entertaining a secret passion for him, but that didn't lead him anywhere. Certainly his idea about Mona Utell had seemed a good one at the time. She was quite capable of calling them up long distance from New York for a joke. It was just the sort of thing she'd do to enliven a party after the evening performance.

But not to end the joke that way. Mona always wanted you laughing with her at the finish.

Perhaps someone else had been playing a joke.

Or perhaps someone else really . . . He shrugged his

shoulders. Such an asinine business. He must tell Tansy. It would amuse her. He started toward the bedroom.

Only then did he remember all that had happened earlier in the evening. The two startling phone calls had quite knocked it out of his head.

He was at the bedroom door. He turned around slowly and looked at the phone. The house was very quiet.

It occurred to him that from one way of looking at it, those two phone calls, coming just when they did, constituted a very unpleasant coincidence.

But a scientist ought to have a healthy disregard for coincidences.

He could hear Tansy breathing softly, regularly.

He switched out the light in the hall and went to bed.

CHAPTER IV

As Norman walked the last block to Hempnell the next morning, it struck him with unusual forcefulness just how pseudo was Hempnell's Gothic. Odd to think how little scholarly thought that ornate architecture masked, and how much anxiety over low salaries and excessive administrative burdens; and among the students, how little passion for knowledge and how much passion, period—even though of a halting, advertisement-derived, movie-stimulated sort. But perhaps that was just what that fabulous gray architecture was supposed to symbolize, even in the old monastic days when its arches and buttresses had been functional.

The walks were empty except for a few hurrying figures, but in three or four minutes the student body would spill out of chapel, a scattering tide of brightly-colored sweaters and jackets.

A delivery van came gliding around the corner as Norman started to cross the street. He stepped back on the curb with a shivery distaste. In this gasoline-obsessed world he didn't mind ordinary automobiles, but somehow trucks with their suggestion of an unwholesome gigantism touched him with a faint irrational horror.

In taking a quick glance around before he started across again, he thought he saw a girl student behind him, either very late for chapel or else cutting it altogether. The next moment he realized that it was Mrs. Carr. He waited for her to catch up with him.

The mistake was a natural one. In spite of her surely seventy years, the silver-haired Dean of Women had a re-markably youthful figure and carriage. Her gait was always brisk and almost supple. Only the second glance revealed the darkened neck, the network of heavy wrinkles, showed you that the slimness was of age not youth. Her manner didn't seem an affectation of girlishness or a pathetic clinging to sex—or, if it were, a very subtle one—but rather a hungry infatuation with youthfulness, with dewiness, with fresh-ness, so great that it influenced the very cells and electrical tensions of her body.

There is a cult of youth among the faculty members of our colleges, Norman began to think, a special form of the great American cult of youth, an almost vampiristic feeding on young eager feelings . . . .

Mrs. Carr's arrival cut him short.

"And *how* is Tansy?" she asked, with such sweet sol-icitude that for a moment Norman wondered if the Dean of Women had even more of an inside wire on the private lives of the faculty than was generally surmised. But only for a moment. After all, sweet solicitude was the Dean of Wo-men's stock-in-trade.

"We missed her at our last faculty wives' meeting," Mrs. Carr continued. "She's such a gay soul. And we *do* need gaiety these days." Cold morning sunlight glinted on her thick glasses and glowed frostily on her apple-red cheeks. She put her hand on his arm. "Hempnell *appreciates* Tansy, Professor Saylor."

Norman's "And why not?" changed to "I think that shows good judgment" as he said it. He derived sardonic amusement from recalling how ten years ago Mrs. Carr was a charter member of *The-Saylors-are-a-demoralizing-influence Club*.

Mrs. Carr's silvery laughter trilled in the chilly air. "I must get on to my student conferences," she said. "But remember, Hempnell appreciates you too, Professor Saylor."

He watched her hurry off, wondering if her last remark meant there had been an unexpected improvement in his chances of getting the vacant chairmanship of the sociology department. Then he turned into Morton Hall.

When he had climbed to his office, the phone was ringing. It was Thompson, who handled Hempnell's public relations—almost the only administrative duty considered too vital to be entrusted to a mere professor.

Thompson's greeting was exceptionally affable. As always, Norman had the vision of a man who would be much happier selling soap. It would take a psychoanalyst, he thought, to discover what weird compulsion made Thompson cling to the fringes of the academic world. We only know that some potentially great salesmen feel impelled to do so.

"A rather delicate matter," Thompson was saying. Delicate matters were one of his fortes. "Just now one of the trustees phoned me. It seems he had heard a very odd story—he wouldn't tell me the source of his information—concerning you and Mrs. Saylor. That over Christmas vacation in New York you had attended a party given by some prominent but . . . er . . . very gay theatrical people. He couldn't be quite straight about where it happened, the party seemed to have wandered all over New York. In fact it all sounded very unlikely. There was something about an impromptu act staged in a night club, and an academic gown, and an . . . er . . . strip-tease dancer. I told him I'd look into it. But naturally I thought . . . and I was wondering if you'd . . ."

"If I'd issue a denial? Sorry, but it wouldn't be honest. The story's substantially true."

"Oh . . . . I see. Well, that's all there is to it then," Thompson answered bravely after a moment. "I thought you'd like to know though. The trustee . . . Fenner . . .

was very hot under the collar. Talked my ear off about how
these particular theatrical people were conspicuous for
drunkenness and divorce.''

"He was right about the former, not the latter. Mona and
Welby Utell are faithful to each other after their fashion. Nice
folk, I'll introduce you to them some time.''

"Oh! . . . That would be interesting, yes,'' replied
Thompson. "Good-by.''

The warning buzzer sounded for classes. Norman stopped
fingering the little obsidian knife he used for slitting envelopes, swiveled his chair away from the desk and leaned
back, amusedly irritated at this latest manifestation of the
Hempnell "hush-hush" policy. Not that he had made any
particular attempt to conceal the Utell party, which had been
a trifle crazier than he had expected. Still, he had said nothing
about it to anyone on campus. No use in being a fool. Now,
after a matter of months, it had all come out anyway.

From where he sat, the roof ridge of Estrey Hall neatly
bisected his office window along the diagonal. There was a
medium-sized cement dragon frozen in the act of clambering
down it. For the tenth time this morning he reminded himself
that what had happened last night had really happened. It was
not so easy. And yet, when you got down to it, Tansy's lapse
into medievalism was not so very much stranger than
Hempnell's architecture, with its sprinkling of gargoyles and
other fabulous monsters designed to scare off evil spirits. The
second buzzer sounded and he got up.

His class in "Primitive Societies" quieted down leisurely
as he strode in. He set a student to explaining the sib as a
factor in tribal organization, then put in the next five minutes
organizing his thoughts and noting late arrivals and absen-
tees. When the explanation, supplemented by blackboard
diagrams of marriage groups, had become so complicated
that Bronstein, the prize student, was twitching with eager-
ness to take a hand, he called for comments and criticisms,
and succeeded in getting a first-class argument going.

Finally the cocksure fraternity president in the second row

said, "But all those ideas of social organization were based on ignorance, tradition and superstition. Unlike modern society."

That was Norman's cue. He lit in joyously, pulverized the defender of modern society with a point-by-point comparison of fraternities and primitive "young men's houses" down to the details of initiation ceremonies, which he dissected with scientific relish, and then launched into a broad analysis of present-day customs as they would appear to a hypothetical ethnologist from Mars. In passing, he drew a facetious analogy between sororities and primitive seclusion of girls at puberty.

The minutes raced pleasantly by as he demonstrated instances of cultural lag in everything from table manners to systems of measurements. Even the lone sleeper in the last row woke up and listened.

"Certainly we've made important innovations, chief among them the systematic use of the scientific method," he said at one point, "but the primitive groundwork is still there, dominating the pattern of our lives. We're modified anthropoid apes inhabiting night clubs and battleships. What else could you expect us to be?"

Marriage and courtship got special attention. With Bronstein grinning delightfully, Norman drew detailed modern parallels to marriage by purchase, marriage by capture, and symbolic marriage to a deity. He showed that trial marriage is no mere modern conception but a well-established ancient custom, successfully practiced by the Polynesians and others.

At this point he became aware of a beet-red, angry face toward the back of the room—that of Gracine Pollard, daughter of Hempnell's president. She glared at him, pointedly ignoring the interest taken by the neighboring students in her blushes.

Automatically it occurred to him, "Now I suppose the little neurotic will be yammering to Papa that Professor Saylor is advocating free love." He shrugged the idea aside

and continued the discussion with modification. The buzzer
cut it short.

But he was feeling irritated with himself. He only half
listened to the enthusiastic comments and questions of Bronstein and a couple of others.

Back at the office he found a note from Harold Gunnison,
the Dean of Men. Having the next hour free, he set out across
the quadrangle for the Administration Building. Bronstein
still tagging along to expound some theory of his own.

But Norman was wondering why he had let himself go.
Admittedly, some of his remarks had been a trifle raw. He
had long ago adjusted his classroom behavior to Hempnell
standards, without losing intellectual integrity, and this
morning's ill-advised though trivial deviation bothered him.

Mrs. Carr swept by him without a word, her face slightly
averted, cutting him cold. A moment later he guessed a
possible explanation. In his abstraction, he had lighted a
cigarette. Moreover, Bronstein had followed suit, obviously
delighted at faculty infraction of a firmly established taboo.
The faculty were only supposed to smoke in their dingy
clubroom or, on the quiet, in their offices.

He frowned, but continued to smoke. Evidently the events
of the previous night had disturbed his mind more than he had
realized. He ground out the butt on the steps of the Administration Building.

In the doorway to the outer office he collided with the
stylishly stout form of Mrs. Gunnison.

"Lucky I had a good hold on my camera," she grumbled,
as he stooped to recover her bulging handbag. "I'd hate to
have to try to replace these lenses." Then brushing back an
untidy wisp of reddish hair from her forehead, "You look
worried. How's Tansy?"

He answered briefly, sliding past her. Now there was a
woman who really ought to be a witch. Expensive clothes
worn sloppily; bossy, snobbish, and gruff; good-humored in
a beefy fashion, but capable of riding rough-shod over anyone else's desires. The only person in whose presence her
husband's authority seemed quite ridiculous.

Harold Gunnison cut short a telephone call and motioned Norman to come in and shut the door.

"Norman," Gunnison began, scowling, "this is a pretty delicate matter."

Norman became attentive. When Harold Gunnison said something was a delicate matter, unlike Thompson, he really meant it. He and Norman played squash together and got on pretty well. Norman's only serious objection to Gunnison was the latter's mutual admiration society with President Pollard, wherein solemn references to Pollard's political ideas and exaggerations of his friendship with national political figures were traded for occasional orotund commendations of the Dean of Men's Office.

But Harold had said, "A delicate matter." Norman braced himself to hear an account of eccentric, indiscreet, or even criminal behavior on the part of Tansy. That suddenly seemed the obvious explanation.

"You have a girl from the Student Employment Agency working for you? A Margaret Van Nice?"

Abruptly Norman realized who had made the second telephone call last night. Covering his shock, he waited a moment and said, "A rather quiet kid. Does mimeographing." Then, with an involuntary look of enlightenment, "Always talks in a whisper."

"Well, a little while ago she threw an hysterical fit in Mrs. Carr's office. Claimed that you had seduced her. Mrs. Carr immediately dumped the whole business in my lap."

Norman fought the impulse to tell about the phone conversation, contented himself with, "Well?"

Gunnison frowned and cocked a sad eye at him.

"I know things like that have happened," Norman said. "Right here at Hempnell. But not this time."

"Of course, Norman."

"Sure. There was opportunity though. We worked late several nights over at Morton."

Gunnison reached for a folder. "On a chance I got out her neurotic index. She ranks way up near the top. A regular bundle of complexes. We'll just have to handle it smoothly."

"I'll want to hear her accuse me," said Norman. "Soon as possible."

"Of course. I've arranged for a meeting at Mrs. Carr's office. Four o'clock this afternoon. Meantime she's seeing Dr. Gardner. That should sober her up."

"Four o'clock," repeated Norman, standing up. "You'll be there?"

"Certainly. I'm sorry about this whole business, Norman. Frankly, I think Mrs. Carr botched it up. Got panicky. She's a pretty old lady."

In the outer office Norman stopped to glance at a small display case of items concerned with Gunnison's work in physical chemistry. The present display was of Prince Rupert drops and other high-tension oddities. He stared moodily at the shiny dark globules with their stiff, twisted tails, vaguely noting the card which told how they were produced by dripping molten glass into hot oil. It occurred to him that Hempnell was something like a Prince Rupert drop. Hit the main body with a hammer and you only jarred your hand. But flick with a fingernail the delicate filament in which the drop ended, and it would explode in your face.

Fanciful.

He glanced at the other objects, among them a tiny mirror which, the legend explained, would fly to powder at the slightest scratch or sudden uneven change in temperature.

Yet it wasn't so fanciful, when you got to thinking about it. Any over-organized, tension-shot, somewhat artificial institution such as a small college tends to develop danger points. And the same would be true of a person or a career. Flick the delicate spot in the mind of a neurotic girl, and she would erupt with wild accusations. Or take a saner person, like himself. Suppose someone were studying him secretly, looking for the vulnerable filament, finger poised to flick—

But that was really getting fanciful. He hurried off to his last morning class.

Coming out of it, Hervey Sawtelle buttonholed him.

Norman's departmental colleague resembled an unfriendly caricature of a college professor. Little older than

Norman, but with the personality of a septuagenarian, or a frightened adolescent. He was always in a hurry, nervous to the point of twitching, and he sometimes carried two brief cases. Norman saw in him one of the all too many victims of intellectual vanity. Very likely during his own college days Hervey Sawtelle had been goaded by arrogant instructors into believing that he ought to know everything about everything, be familiar with all the authorities on all the subjects, including medieval music, differential equations, and modern poetry, be able to produce an instant knowing rejoinder to any conceivable intellectual remark, including those made in dead and foreign languages, and never under any circumstances ask a question. Failing in his subsequent frantic efforts to become much more than a modern Bacon, Hervey Sawtelle had presumably conceived a deep conviction of his intellectual inadequacy, which he tried to conceal, or perhaps forget, by a furious attention to detail.

All this showed in his narrow, shrunken, thin-lipped, high-browed face. Routine worries ceaselessly chased themselves up and down it.

But at the moment he was in the grip of one of his petty excitements.

"Say, Norman, the most interesting thing! I was down in the stakcs this morning, and I happened to pull out an old doctor's thesis—1930—by someone I never heard of—with the title *Superstition and Neurosis.*" He produced a bound, typewritten manuscript that looked as if it had aged without ever being opened. "Almost the same title as your *Parallelisms in Superstition and Neurosis.* An odd coincidence, eh? I'm going to look it over tonight."

They were hurrying together toward the dining hall down a walk flooded with jabbering, laughing students, who curtsied smilingly out of their way. Norman studied Sawtelle's face covertly. Surely the fool must remember that his *Parallelisms* had been published in 1931, giving an ugly suggestion of plagiarism. But Sawtelle's nervous toothy grin was without guile.

He had the impulse to pull Sawtelle aside and tell him that

there was something odder than a coincidence involved, and
that it did not reflect in any way on his own integrity of
scholarship. But this seemed hardly the place.

Yet there was no denying the incident bothered him a
trifle. Why, it was years since he had even thought of that
stupid business of Cunningham's thesis. It had lain buried in
the past—a hidden vulnerability, waiting for the flick of the
fingernail.

Asinine fancifulness! It could all be very well explained,
to Sawtelle or anyone else, at a more suitable time.

Sawtelle's mind was back to habitual anxieties. "You
know, we should be having our conference on the social-
science program for next year. On the other hand, I suppose
we should wait until—" He paused embarrassedly.

"Until it's decided whether you or I get the chairmanship
of the department?" Norman finished for him. "I don't see
why. We'll be working together in any case."

"Yes, of course. I didn't mean to suggest—"

They were joined by some other faculty members on the
steps of the dining hall. The deafening clatter of trays from
the student section was subdued to a slightly fainter din as
they entered the faculty sanctum.

Conversation revolved among the old familiar topics, with
an undercurrent of speculation as to what reorganizations and
expansions of staff the new year might bring to Hempnell.
There was some reference to the political ambitions of Pres-
idnet Pollard—Harold Gunnison confided that a certain
powerful political group was attempting to persuade him to
run for governor; discreet silences here and there around the
table substituted for adverse criticisms on this possibility.
Sawtelle's Adam's apple twitched convulsively at a chance
reference to the vacant chairmanship in sociology.

Norman manged to get a fairly interesting conversation
going, with Holstrom of psychology. He was glad he would
busy with classes and conferences until four o'clock. He
knew he could work half again as hard as someone like
Sawtelle, but if he had to do one quarter of the worrying that
man did—

Yet the four o'clock meeting proved to be an anti-climax. He had no sooner put his hand on the door leading to Mrs. Carr's office, when—as if that had provided the necessary stimulus—a shrill, tearful voice burst out with: "It's all a lie! I made it up!"

Gunnison was sitting near the window, face a trifle averted, arms folded, looking like a slightly bored, slightly embarrassed elephant. In a chair in the center of the room was huddled a delicate, fair-haired girl, tears dribbling down her flat cheeks and hysterical sobs racking her shoulders. Mrs. Carr was trying to calm her in a fluttery way.

"I don't know why I did it," the girl bleated pitifully. "I was in love with him and he wouldn't even look at me. I was going to kill myself last night, and I thought I would do this instead, to hurt him, or—"

"Now, Margaret, you must control yourself," Mrs. Carr admonished, her hands hovering over the girl's shoulders.

"Just a minute," Norman said. "Miss Van Nice—"

She looked around and up at him, apparently just becoming aware of his presence.

Norman waited a little. Neither of them moved. Then he said, "Miss Van Nice, last night between the time you decided to kill yourself and the time you decided to hurt me this way, did you so something else? Did you by any chance make a phone call?"

The girl didn't answer, but after a few moments a blush appeared on her tear-stained face, overspread it, and flowed down under her dress. A little later even her forearms were dull red.

Gunnison registered vague curiosity.

Mrs. Carr looked at the girl sharply, bending toward her. For a moment Norman fancied that there was something distinctly venomous in her searching glance. But that was probably just a trick of the thick glasses, which sometimes magnified Mrs. Carr's eyes until they looked fishlike.

The girl did not react as Mrs. Carr's hands touched her shoulders. She was still looking at Norman, now with an expression of agonized embarrassment and entreaty.

"That's all right," Norman said softly. "Nothing to worry about," and he smiled at her sympathetically.

The girl's expression changed completely. She suddenly shook loose from Mrs. Carr and sprang up facing Norman. "Oh, I hate you!" she screamed. "I hate you!"

Gunnison followed him out of the office. He yawned, shook his head, and remarked, "Glad that's over. Incidentally, Gardner says nothing could possibly have happened to her."

"Never a dull moment," Norman responded, absently.

"Oh, by the way," Gunnison said, dragging a stiff white envelope out of his inside pocket, "here's a note for Mrs. Saylor. Hulda asked me to give it to you. I forgot about it before."

"I met Hulda coming out of your office this morning," Norman said, his thoughts still elsewhere.

Somewhat later, back at Morton, Norman tried to come to grips with those thoughts, but found them remarkably slippery. The dragon on the roof ridge of Estrey Hall lured away his attention. Funny about little things like that. You never even noticed them for years, and then they suddenly popped into focus. How many people could give you one single definite fact about the architectural ornaments of buildings in which they worked? Not one in ten, probably. Why, if you had asked him yesterday about that dragon, he couldn't for his life have been able to tell you even if there was one or not.

He leaned on the window sill, looking at the lizard-like yet grotesquely anthropoid form, bathed in the yellow sunset glow, which, his wandering mind remembered, was supposed to symbolize the souls of the dead passing into and out of the underworld. Below the dragon, jutting from under the cornice, was a sculptured head, one of a series of famous scientists and mathematicians decorating the entablature. He made out the name "Galileo," along with a brief inscription of some sort.

When he turned back to answer the phone, it suddenly seemed very dark in the office.

"Saylor? I just want to tell you that I'm going to give you until tomorrow—"

"Listen, Jennings," Norman cut in sharply, "I hung up on you last night because you kept shouting into the phone. This threatening line won't do you any good."

The voice continued where it had broken off, growing dangerously high. "—until tomorrow to withdraw your charges and have me reinstated at Hempnell."

Then the voice broke into a screaming obscene torrent of abuse, so loud that Norman could still hear it very plainly as he placed the receiver back in the cradle.

Paranoid—that was the way it sounded.

Then he suddenly sat very still.

At twenty past one last night he had burned a charm supposedly designed to ward off evil influence from him. The last of Tansy's "hands."

At about the same time Margaret Van Nice had decided to avow her fanciful passion for him, and Theodore Jennings had decided to make him responsible for an imaginary plot.

Next morning sanctimonious Trustee Fenner had called up Thompson about the Utell party, and Hervey Sawtelle, poking around in the stacks, had found—

Rubbish!

With an angry snort of laughter at his own credulity, he picked up his hat and headed for home.

CHAPTER V

TANSY WAS IN A RADIANT MOOD, prettier than she had seemed in months. Twice he caught her smiling to herself, when he glanced up from his supper.

He gave her the note from Mrs. Gunnison. "Mrs. Carr asked after you, too. Gushed all over me—in a ladylike way, of course. Then, later on—" He caught himself as he started to tell about the cigarette and Mrs. Carr cutting him and the whole Margaret Van Nice business. No use worrying Tansy right now with things that might be considered bad luck. No telling what further construction she might put upon them.

She glanced through the note and handed it back to him.

"It has the authentic Hempnell flavor, don't you think?" she observed.

He read:

Dear Tansy: Where are you keeping yourself? I haven't seen you on campus more than once or twice this last month. If you're busy with something especially interesting, why not tell us about it? Why not come to tea this Saturday, and tell me all about yourself?

Hulda

P.S. You're supposed to bring four dozen cookies to the Local Alumni Wives' Reception the Saturday after.

"Rather confused-sounding," he said, "but I clearly perceive the keen bludgeon of Mrs. Gunnison. She looked particularly sloppy today."

Tansy laughed. "Still, we have been pretty antisocial these last weeks. I believe I'll ask them over for bridge tomorrow night. It's short notice, but they're usually free Wednesdays. And the Sawtelles."

"Do we have to? That henpecker?"

Tansy laughed. "I don't know how you would ever manage to get along without me—" She stopped short. "I'm afraid you'll have to endure Evelyn. After all, Hervey's the other important man in your department, and it's expected that you see something of each other socially. To make two tables, I'll invite the Carrs."

"Three fearful females," said Norman. "If they represent the average run of professors' wives, I was lucky to get you."

"I sometimes think the same thing about professors' wives' husbands," said Tansy.

As they smoked over the coffee, she said hesitatingly, "Norm, I said I didn't want to talk about last night. But now there's something I want to tell you."

He nodded.

"I didn't tell you last night, Norm, but when we burned those . . . things, I was terribly frightened. I felt that we were knocking holes in walls that had taken me years to build, and that now there was nothing to keep out the—"

He said nothing, sat very still.

"Oh, it's hard to explain, but ever since I began to . . . play with those things, I've been conscious of pressure from outside. A vague neurotic fear, something like the way *you* feel about trucks. Things trying to push their way in and get at us. And I've had to press them back, fight back at them with my—It's like that test of strength men sometimes make, trying to force each other's hand to the table. But that wasn't what I was starting to say.

"I went to bed feeling miserable and scared. The pressure from outside kept tightening around me, and I couldn't resist it, because we'd burned those things. And then suddenly, as I lay in the dark, about an hour after I went to bed, I got the most tremendous feeling of relief. The pressure vanished, as if I'd bobbed up to the surface after almost drowning. And I knew then . . . that I'd gotten over my craziness. That's why I'm so happy."

It was hard for Norman not to tell Tansy what he was thinking. Here was one more coincidence, but it knocked the others into a cocked hat. At about the same time as he had burned the last charm, experiencing a sensation of fear, Tansy had felt a great relief. That would teach him to build theories on coincidences!

"For I was crazy in a way, dear," she was saying. "There aren't many people who would have taken it as you did."

He said, "You weren't crazy—which is a relative term, anyway, applicable to anyone. You were just fooled by the cussedness of things."

"Cussedness?"

"Yes. The way nails sometimes insist on bending when you hammer, as if they were trying to. Or the way machinery refuses to work. Matter's funny stuff. In large aggregates, it obeys natural law, but when you get down to the individual atom or electron, it's largely a matter of chance or whim—"
This conversation was not taking the direction he wanted it to, and he was thankful when Totem jumped onto the table, creating a diversion.

It turned out to be the pleasantest evening they had spent together in ages.

But next morning when he arrived at Morton, Norman wished he had not gotten started on that "cussedness of things" notion. It stuck in his mind. He found himself puzzling over the merest trifles—such as the precise position of that idiotic cement dragon. Yesterday he remembered thinking that it was exactly in the middle of the descending roof ridge. But now he saw that it was obviously two thirds of the way down, quite near the architrave topping the huge useless Gothic gateway set between Estrey and Morton. Even a social scientist ought to have better powers of observation than that!

The jangle of the phone coincided with the nine o'clock buzzer.

"Professor Saylor?" Thompson's voice was apologetic. "I'm sorry to bother you again, but I just got another inquiry from one of the trustees—Liddell, this time. Concerning an informal address you were supposed to have delivered at about the same time as that . . . er . . . party. The topic was 'What's wrong with College Education.' "

"Well, what about it? Are you implying there's nothing wrong with college education, or that the topic is taboo?"

"Oh, no, no, no, no. But the trustee seemed to think that you were making a criticism of Hempnell."

"Of small colleges of the same type as Hempnell, yes. Of Hempnell specifically, no."

"Well, he seemed to fear it might have a detrimental effect on enrollment for next year. Spoke of several friends of his with children of college age as having heard your address and being unfavorably impressed."

"Then they were supersensitive."

"He also seemed to think you had made a slighting reference to President Pollard's . . . er . . . political activities."

"I'm sorry but I have to get along to a class now."

"Very well," said Thompson, and hung up. Norman grimaced. The cussedness of things certainly wasn't to be compared with the cussedness of people! Then he jumped up and hurried off to his "Primitive Societies."

Gracine Pollard was absent, he noted with an inward grin, wondering if yesterday's lecture had been too much for her warped sense of propriety. But even the daughters of college presidents ought to be told a few home truths now and then.

And on the others, yesterday's lecture had had a markedly stimulating effect. Several students had abruptly chosen related subjects for their term papers, and the fraternity president had capitalized on his yesterday's discomfiture by planning a humorous article for the Hempnell *Buffoon* on the primitive significance of fraternity initiations. All in all they had a very brisk session.

Afterwards Norman found himself musing good-humoredly on how college students were misunderstood by a great many people.

Collegians were generally viewed as dangerously rebellious and radical, and shockingly experimental in their morality. Indeed the lower classes were inclined to picture them as monsters of unwholesomeness and perversion, potential murderers of little children and celebrants of various equivalents of the Black Mass. Whereas actually they were more conventional than many high school kids. And as for experiments in sex, they were a long way behind those whose education ended with grade school.

Instead of standing up boldly in the classroom and uttering rebel pronouncements, they were much more apt to be fawningly hypocritical, desirous only of saying the thing that would please the teacher most. Small danger of their getting out of hand! On the contrary, it was necessary to charm them slowly into truthfulness, away from the taboos and narrow-mindedness of the home. And how much more complex these problems became, and needful of solution, when you were living in an obvious time of interim morality like today, when national loyalty and faithfulness to family alone were dissolving in favor of a wider loyalty and a wider love—or in favor of a selfish, dog-eat-dog, atom-bombed chaos, if the human spirit were hedged, clipped, and dwarfed by traditional egotisms and fears.

College faculty members were as badly misrepresented to the general public as were college students. Actually they were a pretty timorous folk, exceedingly sensitive to social disapproval. That they occasionally spoke out fearlessly was all the more to their credit.

All of which of course reflected society's slow-dying tendency to view teachers not as educators but as vestal virgins of a sort, living sacrifices on the altar of respectabili-

ty, housed in suitably grim buildings and judged on the basis
of a far stricter moral code than that applied to businessmen
and housewives. And in their vestal-virgining, their virginity
counted much more than their tending of the feeble flame of
imaginative curiosity and honest intellectual inquiry. Indeed,
for all most people cared, the flame might safely be let go
out, so long as the teachers remained sitting around it in their
temple—inviolate, sour-faced, and quite frozen testimonials
to the fact that somebody was upholding moral values somewhere.

Norman thought wryly: Why, they actually *want* us to be
witches, of a harmless sort. And I made Tansy stop!

The irony tickled him and he smiled.

His good humor lasted until after his last class that afternoon, when he happened to meet the Sawtelles in front of
Morton Hall.

Evelyn Sawtelle was a snob and a fake intellectual. The
illusion she tried most to encourage was that she had sac-
rificed a great career in the theater in order to marry Hervey.
While in reality she had never been able to wrangle the
directorship of the Hempnell Student Players and had had to
content herself with a minor position in the speech department. She had an affected carriage and a slightly arty taste in
clothes that, taken along with her flat cheeks and dull black
hair and eyes, suggested the sort of creature you sometimes
see stalking through the lobby at ballet and concert intermis-
sions.

But far from being a bohemian, Evelyn Sawtelle was even
more inclined to agonize over the minutiae of social convention and prestige than most Hempnell faculty wives. Yet
because of her general incompetence, this anxiety did not
result in tactfulness, but rather its opposite.

Her husband was completely under her thumb. She managed him like a business—bunglingly, overzealously, but
with a certain dogged effectiveness.

"I had lunch today with Henrietta . . . I mean Mrs.
Pollard," she announced to Norman with the air of one who
has just visited royalty.

"Oh, say, Norman—" Hervey began excitedly, thrusting forward his brief case.

"We had a very interesting chat," his wife swept on. "We talked about you, too, Norman. It seems Gracine has been misinterpreting some of the things you've been saying in your class. She's such a sensitive girl."

"Dumb bunny, you mean," Norman corrected mentally. He murmured, "Oh?" with some show of politeness.

"Dear Henrietta was a little puzzled as just how to handle it, though of course she's a very tolerant, cosmopolitan soul. I just mentioned it because I thought you'd want to know. After all, it is very important that no one get any wrong impressions about the department. Don't you agree with me, Hervey?" She ended sharply.

"What, dear? Oh, yes, yes. Say, Norman. I want to tell you about that thesis I showed you yesterday. The most amazing thing! Its main arguments are almost the same as those in your book! An amazing case of independent investigators arriving at the same conclusions. Why, it's like Darwin and Wallace, or—"

"You didn't tell *me* anything about this, dear," said his wife.

"Wait a minute," said Norman.

He hated to make an explanation in Mrs. Sawtelle's presence, but it had to be done.

"Sorry, Hervey, to have to substitute a rather sordid story for an intriguing scientific coincidence. It happened when I was an instructor here—1929, my first year. A graduate student named Cunningham got hold of my ideas—I was friendly with him—and incorporated them into his doctor's thesis. My work in superstition and neurosis was just a side line then, and partly because I was sick with pneumonia for two months I didn't read his thesis until after he'd gotten his degree."

Sawtelle blinked. He face resumed its usual worried expression. A look of vague disappointment came into Mrs. Sawtelle's black-button eyes, as she would have liked to read the thesis, lingering over each paragraph, letting her suspicions have full scope, before hearing the explanation.

"I was very angry," Norman continued, "and intended to expose him. But then I heard he'd died. There was some hint of suicide. He was an unbalanced chap. How he'd hoped to get away with such an out-and-out steal, I don't know. Anyway, I decided not to do anything about it, for his family's sake. You see, it would have supplied a reason for thinking he *had* committed suicide."

Mrs. Sawtelle looked incredulous.

"But, Norman," Sawtelle commented anxiously, "was that really wise? I mean to keep silent. Weren't you taking a chance? I mean with regard to your academic reputation?"

Abruptly, Mrs. Sawtelle's manner changed.

"Put that thing back in the stacks, Hervey, and forget about it," she directed curtly. Then she smiled archly at Norman. "I've been forgetting I have a surprise for you, Professor Saylor. Come down to the sound booth now, and I'll show you. It won't take a minute. Come along, Harvey."

Norman had no excuse ready, so he accompanied the Sawtelles to the rooms of the speech department at the other end of Morton, wondering how the speech department ever found any use for someone with as nasal and affected a voice as Evelyn Sawtelle, even if she did happen to be a professor's wife and a thwarted tragedienne.

The sound booth was dim and quiet, a solid box with sound-resistant walls and double windows. Mrs. Sawtelle took a disk from the cabinet, put it on one of the three turntables, and adjusted a couple of dials. Norman jerked. For an instant he thought that a truck was roaring toward the sound booth and would momentarily crash through the insulating walls. Then the abominable noise pouring from the amplifier changed to a strangely pulsing wail or whir, as of wind prying at a house. It struck a less usual chord, though, in Norman's agitated memory.

Mrs. Sawtelle darted back and swiveled the dials.

"I made a mistake," she said. "That's some modernistic music or other. Hervey, switch on the light. Here's the record I wanted." She put it on one of the other turntables.

"It sounded awful, whatever it was," her husband observed.

Norman had identified his memory. It was of an Australian bull-roarer a colleague had once demonstrated for him. The curved slat of wood, whirled at the end of a cord, made exactly the same sound. The aborigines used it in their rain magic.

" . . . but if, in these times of misunderstanding and strife, we willfully or carelessly forget that every word and thought must refer to something in the real world, if we allow references to the unreal and the nonexistent to creep into our minds . . ."

Again Norman started. For now it was his own voice that was coming out of the amplifier and he had an odd sense of jerking back in time.

"Surprised?" Evelyn Sawtelle questioned coyly. "It's that talk on semantics you gave the students last week. We had a mike spotted by the speaker's rostrum—I suppose you thought it was for amplification—and we made a sneak recording, as we call it. We cut it down here."

She indicated the heavier, cement-based turn-table for making recordings. Her hands fluttered around the dials.

"We can do all sorts of things down here," she babbled on. "Mix all sorts of sounds. Music against voices. And—"

"Words *can* hurt us, you know. And oddly enough, it's the words that refer to things that *aren't*, that can hurt us most. Why . . ."

It was hard for Norman to appear even slightly pleased. He knew his reasons were no more sensible than those of a savage afraid someone will learn his secret name, yet all the same he disliked the idea of Evelyn Sawtelle monkeying around with his voice. Like her dully malicious, small-socketed eyes, it suggested a prying for hidden weaknesses.

And then Norman moved involuntarily for a third time. For suddenly out of the amplifier, but now mixed with his voice, came the sound of the bull-roarer that still had that devilish hint of an onrushing truck.

"Oh, there I've done it again," said Evelyn Sawtelle

rapidly, snatching at the dials. "Messing up your beautiful voice with that terrible music." She grimaced. "But then, as you just said, Professor Saylor, sounds can't hurt us."

Norman did not correct her typical misquoting. He looked at her curiously for a moment. She stood facing him, her hands behind her. Her husband, his nose twitching, had idled over to the still moving turntables and was gingerly poking a finger at one of them.

"No," said Norman slowly, "they can't." And then he excused himself with a brusque, "Well, thanks for the demonstration."

"We'll see you tonight," Evelyn called after him. Somehow it sounded like, "You won't get rid of me."

How I detest that woman, thought Norman, as he hurried up the dark stair and down the corridor.

Back at his office, he put in a good hour's work on his notes. Then getting up to switch on the light, his glance happened to fall on the window.

After a few moments, he jerked away and darted to the closet to get his field glasses.

Someone must have a very obscure sense of humor to perpetrate such a complicated practical joke.

Intently he searched the cement at the juncture of roof ridge and clawed feet, looking for the telltale cracks. He could not spot any, but that would not have been easy in the failing yellow light.

The cement dragon now stood at the edge of the gutter, as if about to walk over to Morton along the architrave of the big gateway.

He lifted his glasses to the creature's head—blank and crude as an unfinished skull. Then on an impulse he dropped down to the row of sculptured heads, focused on Galileo, and read the little inscription he had not been able to make out before.

"*Eppur si muove.*"

The words Galileo was supposed to have muttered after recanting before the Inquisition his belief in the revolution of the earth around the sun.

"Nevertheless, it moves."

A board creaked behind him, and he spun around.

By his desk stood a young man, waxen pale, with thick red hair. His eyes stood out like milky marbles. One white, tendon-ridged hand gripped a .22 target pistol.

Norman walked toward him, bearing slightly to the right.

The skimpy barrel of the gun came up.

"Hullo, Jennings," said Norman. "You've been reinstated. Your grades have been changed to straight A's."

The gun barrel slowed for an instant.

Norman lunged in.

The gun went off under his left arm, pinking the window.

The gun clunked on the floor. Jennings' skinny form went limp. As Norman sat him down on the chair, he began to sob, convulsively.

Norman picked up the gun by the barrel, laid it in a drawer, locked the drawer, pocketed the key. Then he lifted the phone and asked for an on-campus number. The connection was made quickly. "Gunnison?" he asked.

"Uh-huh, just caught me as I was leaving."

"Theodore Jennings' parents live right near the college, don't they? You know, the chap who flunked out last semester."

"Of course they do. What's the matter?"

"Better get them over here quick. And have them bring his doctor. He just tried to shoot me. Yes, *his* doctor. No, neither of us is hurt. But quickly."

Norman put down the phone. Jennings continued to sob agonizingly. Norman looked at him with disgust for a moment, then patted his shoulder.

An hour later Gunnison sat down in the same chair, and let off a sigh of relief.

"I'm sure glad they agreed about asking for his commitment to the asylum," he said. "It was awfully good of you, Norman, not to insist on the police. Things like that give a college a bad name."

Norman smiled wearily. "Almost anything gives a college a bad name. But that kid was obviously as crazy as a loon.

And of course I understand how much the Jenningses, with their political connections and influence, mean to Pollard.''

Gunnison nodded. The lit up and smoked for a while in silence. Norman thought how different real life was from a detective story, where an attempted murder was generally considered a most serious thing, an occasion for much turmoil and telephoning and the gathering of flocks of official and unofficial detectives. Whereas here, because it occurred in an area of life governed by respectability rather than sensation, it was easily hushed up and forgotten.

Gunnison looked at his watch. ''I'll have to hustle. It's almost seven, and we're due at your place at eight.''

But he lingered, ambling over to the window to inspect the bullet hole.

''I wonder if you'd mind not mentioning this to Tansy?'' Norman asked. ''I don't want to worry her.''

Gunnison nodded. ''Good thing if we kept it to ourselves.'' Then he pointed out the window. ''That's one of my wife's pets,'' he remarked in a jocular tone.

Norman saw that his finger was trained on the cement dragon, now coldly revealed by the upward glare from the street lights.

''I mean,'' Gunnison went on, ''she must have a dozen photographs of it. Hempnell's her specialty. I believe she's got a photograph of every architectural oddity on campus. That one is her favorite.'' He chuckled. ''Usually it's the husband who keeps ducking down into the darkroom, but not in our family. And me a chemist, at that.''

Norman's taut mind had unaccountably jumped to the thought of a bull-roarer. Abruptly he realized the analogy between the recording of a bull-roarer and the photograph of a dragon.

He clamped a lid on the fantastic questions he wanted to ask Gunnison.

''Come on!'' he said. ''We'd better get along.''

Gunnison started a little at the harshness of his voice.

''Can you drop me off?'' asked Norman in quieter tones. ''My car's at home.''

"Sure thing," said Gunnison.

After he switched out the lights, Norman paused for a moment, staring at the window. The words came back.

"Eppur si muove."

CHAPTER VI

THEY HAD HARDLY CLEARED away the remains of a hasty supper, when there came the first clang from the front-door chimes. To Norman's relief, Tansy had accepted without questioning his rather clumsy explanation of why he had gotten home so late. There was something puzzling, though, about her serenity these last two days. She was usually much sharper and more curious. But of course he had been careful to hide disturbing events from her, and he ought only to be glad her nerves were in such good shape.

"Dearest! It's been *ages* since we've seen you!" Mrs. Carr embraced Tansy cuddlingly. "How are you? How are you?" The question sounded peculiarly eager and incisive. Norman put it down to typical Hempnell gush. "Oh, dear, I'm afraid I've got a cinder in my eye," Mrs. Carr continued. "The wind's getting quite fierce."

"Gusty," said Professor Carr of the mathematics department, showing harmless delight at finding the right word. He was a little man with red cheeks and a white Vandyke, as innocent and absent-minded as college professors are supposed to be. He gave the impression of residing permanently in a special paradise of transcendental and transfinite num-

59

bers and of the hieroglyphs of symbolic logic, for whose manipulations he had a nationally recognized fame among mathematicians. Russell and Whitehead may have invented those hieroglyphs, but when it came to handling, cherishing, and coaxing the exasperating, riddlesome things, Carr was the champion prestidigitator.

"It seems to have gone away now," said Mrs. Carr, waving aside Tansy's handkerchief and experimentally blinking her eyes, which looked unpleasantly naked until she replaced her thick glasses. "Oh, that must be the others," she added, as the chimes sounded. "Isn't it *marvelous* that everyone at Hempnell is so punctual?"

As Norman started for the front door he imagined for the crazy moment that someone must be whirling a bull-roarer outside, until he realized it could only be the rising wind living up to Professor Carr's description of it.

He was confronted by Evelyn Sawtelle's angular form, wind whipping her black coat against her legs. Her equally angular face, with its shoe-button eyes, was thrust toward his own.

"Let us in, or it'll blow us in," she said. Like most of her attempts at coy or facetious humor, it did not come off, perhaps because she made it sound so stupidly grim. She entered, with Hervey in tow, and made for Tansy.

"My dear, how are you? Whatever have you been doing with yourself?" Again Norman was struck by the eager and meaningful tone of the question. For a moment he wondered whether the woman had somehow gotten an inkling of Tansy's eccentricity and the recent crisis. But Mrs. Sawtelle was so voice-conscious that she was always emphasizing things the wrong way.

There was a noisy flurry of greetings, Totem squeaked and darted out of the way of the crowd of human beings. Mrs. Carr's voice rose above the rest, shrilling girlishly.

"Oh, Professor Sawtelle, I want to tell you how *much* we appreciated your talk on city planning. It was truly *significant*!" Sawtelle writhed.

Norman thought: "So now *he's* the favorite for the chairmanship."

Professor Carr had made a beeline for the bridge tables and was wistfully fingering the cards.

"I've been studying the mathematics of the shuffle," he began with a bright-eyed air, as soon as Norman drifted into range. "The shuffle is supposed to make it a matter of chance what hands are dealt. But that is not true at all." He broke open a new pack of cards and spread the deck. "The manufacturers arrange these by suits—thirteen spades, thirteen hearts, and so on. Now suppose I make a perfect shuffle—divide the pack into equal parts and interleaf the cards one by one."

He tried to demonstrate, but the cards got away from him.

"It's really not as hard as it looks," he continued amiably. "Some players can do it every time, quick as a wink. But that's not the point. Suppose I make two perfect shuffles with a new pack. Then, no matter how the cards are cut, each player will get thirteen of a suit—an event that, if you went purely by the laws of chance, would happen only once in about one hundred and fifty-eight billion times as regards a *single* hand, let alone all four."

Norman nodded and Carr smiled delightedly.

"That's only one example. It comes to this: What is loosely termed chance is really the resultant of several perfectly definite factors—chiefly the play of cards on each hand, and the shuffle-habits of the players." He made it sound as important as the Theory of Relativity. "Some evenings the hands are very ordinary. Other evenings they keep getting wilder and wilder—long suits, voids and so on. Sometimes the cards persistently run north and south. Other times, east and west. Luck? Chance? Not at all! It's the result of known causes. Some expert players actually make use of this principle to determine the probably location of key cards. They remember how the cards were played on the last hand, how the packets were put together, how the shuffle-habits of the maker have disarranged the cards. Then they interpret

that information according to the bids and opening leads the
next time the cards are used. Why, it's really quite simple—
or would be for a blindfolded chess expert. And of course any
really good bridge player should—''

Norman's mind went off at a tangent. Suppose you applied
this principle outside bridge? Suppose that coincidence and
other chance happenings weren't really as chancy as they
looked? Suppose there were individuals with a special ap-
titude for calling the turns, making the breaks? But that was a
pretty obvious idea—nothing to give a person the shiver it
had given him.

"I wonder what's holding up the Gunnisons," Professor
Carr was saying. "We might start one table now. Perhaps we
can get in an extra rubber," he added hopefully.

A peal from the chimes settled the question.

Gunnison looked as if he had eaten his dinner too fast and
Hulda seemed rather surly.

"We had to rush so," she muttered curtly to Norman as he
held open the door.

Like the other two women, she almost ignored him and
concentrated her greetings on Tansy. It gave him a vaguely
uneasy feeling as when they had first come to Hempnell and
faculty visits had been a nerve-racking chore. Tansy seemed
at a disadvantage, unprotected, in contrast to the aggressive
air animating the other three.

But what of it?—he told himself. That was normal for
Hempnell faculty wives. They acted as if they lay awake
nights plotting to poison the people between their husbands
and the president's chair.

Whereas Tansy—But that was like what Tansy had been
doing or rather what Tansy had said *they* were doing. *She*
hadn't been doing it. She had only been—His thoughts
started to gyrate confusingly and he switched them off.

They cut for partners.

The cards seemed determined to provide an illustration for
the theory Carr had explained. The hands were uniformly
commonplace—abnormally average. No long suits. Nothing

but 4-4-3-2 and 4-3-3-3 distribution. Bid one; make two. Bid two; down one.

After the second round, Norman applied his private remedy for boredom—the game of "Spot the Primitive." You played it by yourself, secretly. It was just an exercise for an ethnologist's imagination. You pretended that the people around you were members of a savage race, and you tried to figure out how their personalities would manifest themselves in such an environment.

Tonight it worked almost too well.

Nothing unusual about the men. Gunnison, of course, would be a prosperous tribal chieftain; perhaps a little fatter, and tended by maidens, but with a jealous and vindictive wife waiting to pounce. Carr might figure as the basket maker of the village—a spry old man, grinning like a little monkey, weaving the basket fibers into intricate mathematical matrices. Sawtelle, of course, would be the tribal scapegoat, butt of endless painful practical jokes.

But the women!

Take Mrs. Gunnison, now his partner. Give her a brown skin. Leave the red hair, but twist some copper ornaments in it. She'd be heftier if anything, a real mountain of a woman, stronger than most of the men in the tribe, able to wield a spear or club. The same brutish eyes, but the lower lip would jut out in a more openly sullen and domineering way. It was only too easy to imagine what she'd do to the unlucky maidens in whom her husband showed too much interest. Or how she would pound tribal policy into his head when they retired to their hut. Or how her voice would thunder out the death chants the women sang to aid the men away at war.

Then Mrs. Sawtelle and Mrs. Carr, who had progressed to the top table along with himself and Mrs. Gunnison. Mrs. Sawtelle first. Make her skinnier, Scarify the flat cheeks with ornamental ridges. Tattoo the spine. Witch woman. Bitter as quinine bark because her husband was ineffectual. Think of her prancing before a spike-studded fetish. Think of her screeching incantations and ripping off a chicken's head . . .

"Norman, you are playing out of turn," said Mrs. Gunnison.

"Sorry."

And Mrs. Carr. Shrivel her a bit. Leave only a few wisps of hair on the parchment skull. Take away the glasses, so her eyes would be gummy. She'd blink and peer short-sightedly, and leer toothlessly, and flutter her bony claws. A nice harmless old squaw, who'd gather the tribe's children around her (always that hunger for youth!) and tell them legends. But her jaw would still be able to snap like a steel trap, and her clawlike hands would be deft at applying arrow poison, and she wouldn't really need her eyes because she'd have other ways of seeing things, and even the bravest warrior would grow nervous if she looked too long in his direction.

"Those experts at the top table are awfully quiet," called Gunnison with a laugh. "They must be taking the game very seriously."

Witch women, all three of them, engaged in booting their husbands to the top of the tribal hierarchy.

From the dark doorway at the far end of the room, Totem was peering curiously as if weighing some similar possibility.

But Norman could not fit Tansy into the picture. He could visualize physical changes, like frizzing her hair and putting some big rings in her ears and a painted design on her forehead. But he could not picture her as belonging to the same tribe. She persisted in his imagination as a stranger woman, a captive, eyed with suspicion and hate by the rest. Or perhaps a woman of the same tribe, but one who had done something to forfeit the trust of all the other women. A priestess who had violated taboo. A witch who had renounced witchcraft.

Abruptly his field of vision narrowed to the score pad. Evelyn Sawtelle was idly scribbling stick figures as Mrs. Carr deliberated over a lead. First the stick figure of a man with arms raised and three or four balls above his head, as if he were juggling. Then the stick figure of a queen, indicated by crown and skirt. Then a little tower with battlements. Then an L-shaped thing with a stick figure hanging from it—a gallows. Finally, a crude vehicle—a rectangle with two wheels—bearing down on a man whose arms were extended toward it in fear.

Just five scribbles. But Norman knew that four of them were connected with a bit of unusual knowledge buried somewhere in his mind. A glance at the exposed dummy gave him the clue.

Cards.

But this bit of knowledge was from the ancient history of cards, when the whole deck was drenched with magic, when there was a Knight between the Jack and Queen, when the suits were swords, batons, cups, and money, and when there were twenty-two special tarot, or fortune-telling, cards in the pack, of which today only the Joker remained.

But Evelyn Sawtelle knowing about anything so recondite as tarot cards? Knowing them so well she doodled them? Stupid, affected, conventional Evelyn Sawtelle? It was unthinkable. Yet—four of the tarot cards were the Juggler, the Empress, the Tower, and the Hanged Man.

Only the fifth stick figure, that of the man and vehicle, did not fit in. Juggernaut? The fanatical, finally cringing victim about to die under the wheels of the vast, trundling idol? That was closer—and chalk one more up to the esoteric scholarship of stupid Evelyn Sawtelle.

Suddenly it came to him. Himself and a truck. A great big truck. That was the meaning of the fifth stick figure.

But Evelyn Sawtelle knowing his pet phobia?

He stared at her. She scratched out the stick figures and looked at him sullenly.

Mrs. Gunnison leaned forward, lips moving as if she might be counting trump.

Mrs. Carr smiled, and made her lead. The risen wind began to make the same intermittent roaring sound it had for a moment earlier in the evening.

Norman suddenly chuckled whistlingly, so that the three

women looked at him. Why, what a fool he was! Worrying about witchcraft, when all Evelyn Sawtelle had been doodling was a child playing ball—the child she couldn't have; a stick queen—herself; a tower—her husband's office as chairman of the sociology department, or some other and more fundamental potency; a hanged man—Hervey's impotence (that was an idea!); fearful man and truck—her own sexual energy horrifying and crushing Hervey.

He chuckled again, so that the three women lifted their eyebrows. He looked around at them enigmatically.

"And yet," he asked himself, continuing his earlier ruminations, in what was, at first, a much lighter vein, "why not?"

Three witch women using magic as Tansy had, to advance their husbands' careers and their own.

Making use of their husbands' special knowledge to give magic a modern twist. Suspicious and worried because Tansy had given up magic; afraid she'd found a much stronger variety and was planning to make use of it.

And Tansy—suddenly unprotected, possibly unaware of the change in their attitude toward her because, in giving up magic, she had lost her sensitivity to the super-natural, her "woman's intuition."

Why not carry it a step further? Maybe all women were the same. Guardians of mankind's ancient customs and traditions, including the practice of witchcraft. Fighting their husbands' battles from behind the scenes, by sorcery. Keeping it a secret; and on those occasions when they were discovered, conveniently explaining it as feminine susceptibility to superstitious fads.

Half of the human race still actively practicing sorcery. Why not?

"It's your play, Norman," said Mrs. Sawtelle, sweetly.

"You look as if you had something on your mind," said Mrs. Gunnison.

"How are you getting along up there, Norm?" her husband called. "Those women got you buffaloed?"

Buffaloed? Norman came back to reality with a jerk. That was just what they almost had done. And all because the human imagination was a thoroughly unreliable instrument, like a rubber ruler. Let's see, if he played his King it might set up a Queen in Mrs. Gunnison's hand so she could get in and run her spades.

As Mrs. Carr topped it with her ace, Norm was conscious of her wrinkled lips fixed in a faint cryptic smile.

After that hand, Tansy served refreshments. Norman followed her to the kitchen.

"Did you see the looks she kept giving you?" she whispered gaily to Norman. "I sometimes think the bitch is in love with you."

He chuckled. "You mean Evelyn?"

"Of course not. Mrs. Carr. Inside she's a glamor girl. Haven't you ever seen her looking at the students, wishing she had the outside too?"

Norman remembered he'd been thinking the very thing that morning.

Tansy continued, "I'm not trying to flatter myself when I say I've caught her looking at me in the same way. It gives me the creeps."

Norman nodded. "She reminds me of the Wicked—" he caught himself.

"—Witch in Snow White? Yes. And now you'd better run along, dear, or they'll be bustling out here to remind me that a Hempnell man's place is definitely not in the kitchen."

When he returned to the living room, the usual shop talk had started.

"Saw Pollard today," Gunnison remarked, helping himself to a section of chocolate cake. "Told me he'd be meeting with the trustees tomorrow morning, to decide among other things on the sociology chairmanship."

Hervey Sawtelle choked on a crumb and almost upset his cup of cocoa.

Norman caught Mrs. Sawtelle glaring at him vindictively. She changed her face and murmured, "How interesting."

He smiled. That kind of hate he could understand. No need to confuse it with witchcraft.

He went to the kitchen to get Mrs. Carr a glass of water, and met Mrs. Gunnison coming out of the bedroom. She was slipping a leather bound booklet into her capacious handbag. It recalled to his mind Tansy's diary. Probably an address book.

Totem slipped out from behind her, hissing decorously as she dodged past her feet.

"I loathe cats," said Mrs. Gunnison bluntly and walked past him.

Professor Carr had made arrangements for a final rubber, men at one table, women at the other.

"A barbaric arrangement," said Tansy, winking. "You really don't think we can play bridge at all."

"On the contrary, my dear, I think you play very well," Carr replied seriously. "But I confess that at times I prefer to play with men. I can get a better idea of what's going on in their minds. Whereas women still baffle me."

"As they should, dear," added Mrs. Carr, bringing a flurry of laughter.

The cards suddenly began to run freakishly, with abnormal distribution of suits, and play took a wild turn. But Norman found it impossible to concentrate, which made Sawtelle an even more jittery partner than usual.

He kept listening to what the women were saying at the other table. His rebellious imagination persisted in reading hidden meanings into the most innocuous remarks.

"You usually hold wonderful hands, Tansy. But tonight you don't seem to have any," said Mrs. Carr. But suppose she was referring to the kind of hand you wrapped in flannel?

"Oh, well, unlucky in cards . . . you know." How had Mrs. Sawtelle meant to finish the remark? Lucky in love? Lucky in sorcery? Idiotic notion!

"That's two psychic bids you've made in succession, Tansy. Better watch out. We'll catch up with you." What might not a psychic bid stand for in Mrs. Gunnison's vocabulary? Some kind of bluff in witchcraft? A pretense at giving up conjuring?

"I wonder," Mrs. Carr murmured sweetly to Tansy, "if you're hiding a very strong hand this time, dear, and making a trap pass?"

Rubber ruler. That was the trouble with imagination. According to a rubber ruler, an elephant would be no bigger than a mouse, a jagged line and a curve might be equally straight. He tried to think about the slam he had contracted for.

"The girls talk a good game of bridge," murmured Gunnison in an undertone.

Gunnison and Carr came out at the long end of a two-thousand rubber and were still crowing pleasantly as they stood around waiting to leave.

Norman remembered a question he wanted to ask Mrs. Gunnison.

"Harold was telling me you had a number of photographs of that cement dragon or whatever it is on top of Estrey. It's right opposite my window."

She looked at him for a moment, then nodded.

"I believe I've got one with me. Took it almost a year ago."

She dug a rumpled snapshot out of her handbag.

He studied it, and experienced a kind of shiver in reverse. This didn't make sense at all. Instead of being toward the center of the roof ridge, or near the bottom, it was almost at the top. Just what was involved here? A practical joke stretching over a period of days or weeks? Or—His mind balked, like a skittish horse. Yet—*Eppur si muove.*

He turned it over. There was a confusing inscription on the back, in greasy red crayon. Mrs. Gunnison took it out of his hands, to show the others.

"The wind sounds like a lost soul," said Mrs. Carr, hugging her coat around her as Norman opened the door.

"But a rather talkative one—probably a woman," her husband added with a chuckle.

When the last of them were gone, Tansy slipped her arm

around his waist, and said, ''I must be getting old. It wasn't nearly as much of a trial as usual. Even Mrs. Carr's ghoulish flirting didn't bother me. For once they all seemed almost human.''

Norman looked down at her intently. She was smiling peacefully. Totem had come out of hiding and was rubbing against her legs.

With an effort Norman nodded and said, ''Yes, they did. But God, that cocoa! Let's have a drink!''

CHAPTER VII

THERE WERE SHADOWS EVERYWHERE, and the ground under Norman's feet was soft and quivering. The dreadful strident roaring, which seemed to have gone on since eternity began, shook his very bones. Yet it did not drown out the flat, nasty monotone of that other voice which kept telling him to do something—he could not be sure what, except that it involved injury to himself, although he heard the voice as plainly as if someone were talking inside his head. He tried to struggle away from the direction in which the voice wanted him to go, but heavy hands jerked him back. He wanted to look over his shoulder at something he knew would be taller than himself, but he couldn't muster the courage. The shadows were made by great rushing clouds which would momentarily assume the form of gigantic faces brooding down on him, faces with pits of darkness for eyes, and sullen, savage lips, and great masses of hair streaming behind.

He must not do the thing the voice commanded. And yet he must. He struggled wildly. The sound rose to an earth-shaking pandemonium. The clouds became a black all-engulfing torrent.

And then suddenly the bedroom became mixed up with the other picture, and he struggled awake.

He rubbed his face, which was thick with sleep, and tried unsuccessfully to remember what the voice had wanted him to do. He still felt the reverberations of the sound in his ears.

Gloomy daylight seeped through the shades. The clock indicated quarter to eight.

Tansy was still curled up, one arm out of the covers. A smile was tickling the corners of her lips and wrinkling her nose. Norman slipped out carefully. His bare foot came down on a loose carpet tack. Suppressing an angry grunt, he hobbled off.

For the first time in months he botched shaving. Twice the new blade slid too sharply sideways, neatly removing tiny segments of skin. He glared irritably at the white-glazed, red-flecked face in the mirror, pulled the blade down his chin very slowly, but with a little too much pressure, and gave himself a third nick.

By the time he got down to the kitchen, the water he had put on was boiling. As he poured it into the coffeepot, the wobbly handle of the saucepan came completely loose, and his bare ankles were splattered painfully. Totem skittered away, then slowly returned to her pan of milk. Norman cursed, then grinned. What had he been telling Tansy about the cussedness of things? As if to prove the point with a final ridiculous example, he bit his tongue while eating coffee cake. Cussedness of things? Say rather the cussedness of the human nervous system! Faintly he was aware of a potently disturbing and unidentifiable emotion—remnant of the dream?—like an unpleasant swimming shape glimpsed beneath weedy water.

It seemed most akin to a dull seething anger, for as he hurried toward Morton Hall, he found himself inwardly at war with the established order of things, particularly educational institutions. The old sophomoric exasperation at the hypocrisies and compromises of civilized society welled up and poured over the dams that a mature realism had set against it. This was a great life for a man to be leading! Coddling the immature minds of grownup brats, and lucky to get one halfway promising student a year. Playing bridge with a bunch of old fogies. Catering to jittery incompetents like Hervey Sawtelle. Bowing to the thousand and one stupid rules and traditions of a second-rate college. And for what!

Ragged clouds were moving overhead, presaging rain. They reminded him of his dream. He felt the impulse to shout a childish defiance at those faces in the sky.

A truck rolled quietly by, recalling to his mind the little picture Evelyn Sawtelle had scribbled on the bridge pad. He followed it with his eyes. When he turned back, he saw Mrs. Carr.

"You've cut yourself," she said with sweet solicitude, peering sharply through her spectacles.

"Yes, I have."

"How unfortunate!"

He didn't even agree. They walked together through the gate between Estrey and Morton. He could just make out the snout of the cement dragon poked over the Estrey gutter.

"I wanted to tell you last night how distressed I was, Professor Saylor, about the matter of Margaret Van Nice, only of course, it wasn't the right time. I'm dreadfully sorry that you had to be called in. Such a disgusting accusation! How you must have felt!"

She seemed to misinterpret his wry grimace at this, for she went on very swiftly, "Of course, I never once dreamed that *you* had done anything the least improper, but I thought there must be *something* to the girl's story. She told it in such *detail*." She studied his face with interest. The thick glass made her eyes big as an owl's. "Really, Professor Saylor, some of the girls that come to Hempnell nowadays are *terrible*. Where they get such loathsome ideas from is quite beyond me."

"Would you like to know?"

She looked at him blankly, an owl in daytime.

"They get them," he told her concisely, "from a society.

which seeks simultaneously to stimulate and inhibit one of their basic drives. They get them, in brief, from a lot of dirty-minded adults!''

"Really, Professor Saylor! Why—''

"There are a number of girls here at Hempnell who would be a lot healthier with real love affairs rather than imaginary ones. A fair proportion, of course, have already made satisfactory adjustments.''

He had the satisfaction of hearing her gasp as he abruptly turned into Morton. His heart was pounding pleasantly. His lips were tight. When he reached his office he lifted his phone and asked for an on-campus number.

"Thompson? . . . Saylor. I have a couple of news items for you.''

"Good, good! What are they?'' Thompson replied hungrily, in the tone of one who poises a pencil.

"First, the subject for my address to the Off-campus Mothers, week after next: 'Pre-marital Relations and the College Student.' Second, my theatrical friends—the Utells—will be playing in the city at the same time, and I shall invite them to be guests of the college.''

"But—'' The poised pencil had obviously been stopped like a red-hot poker.

"That's all, Thompson. Perhaps I shall have something more interesting another time. Goodby.''

He felt a stinging sensation in his hand. He had been fingering the little obsidian knife. It had gashed his finger. Blood smeared the clear volcanic glass where once, he told himself, had been the blood of sacrifice or ritual scarification. Clumsy—he searched his desk for adhesive bandages. The drawer where he remembered putting them was locked. He opened it and there was the slim-barreled revolver he had taken from Theodore Jennings. The buzzer sounded. He shut the drawer, locked it again, ripped a strip of cloth from his handkerchief, and hurriedly tied it around the dripping wound.

As he hurried down the corridor, Bronstein fell into step with him.

"We're pulling for you this morning, Dr. Saylor," he murmured heartily.

"What do you mean?"

Bronstein's grin was a trifle knowing. "A girl who works in the president's office told us they were deciding on the sociology chairmanship. I sure hope the old buzzards show some sense for once."

Academic dignity stiffened Norman's reply. "In any case, I will be satisfied with their decision."

Bronstein felt the rebuff. "Of course, I didn't mean to—"

"Of course you didn't."

He immediately regretted his sharpness. Why the devil should he rebuke a student for failing to reverence trustees as representatives of deity? Why pretend he didn't want the chairmanship? Why conceal his contempt for half the faculty? The anger he thought he had worked out of his system surged up with redoubled violence. On a sudden irresistible impulse he tossed his lecture notes aside and started in to tell the class just what he thought of the world and Hempnell. They might as well find out young!

Fifteen minutes later he came to with a jerk in the middle of a sentence about "dirty-minded old women, in whom greed for social prestige has reached the magnitude of a perversion." He could not remember half of what he had been saying. He searched the faces of his class. They looked excited, but puzzled, most of them, and a few looked shocked. Gracine Pollard was glaring. Yes! He remembered now that he had made a neat but nasty analysis of the political ambitions of a certain college president who could be none other than Randolph Pollard. And somewhere he had started off on that pre-marital relations business, and had been ribald about it, to say the least. And he had—

Exploded. Like a Prince Rupert drop.

He finished off with half a dozen lame generalities. He knew they must be quite inappropriate, for the looks grew more puzzled.

But the class seemed very remote. A shiver was spreading downward from the base of his skull, all because of a few words that had printed themselves in his mind.

The words were: A fingernail has flicked a psychic filament.

He shook his head, jumbling the type. The words vanished.

There were thirty minutes of class time left. He wanted to get away. He announced a surprise quiz, chalked up two questions, and left the room. In his office, he noticed that the cut finger had started to bleed again through the bandage. He remembered that there had been blood on the chalk.

And dried blood on the obsidian knife. He resisted the impulse to finger it, and sat staring at the top of his desk.

It all went back to Tansy's witchcraft aberration, he told himself. It had shaken him much more than he had dared to admit. He had tried to put it out of his mind too quickly. And Tansy had appeared to forget it too quickly. He must thrash it all out with her, again, and again, or the thing would fester.

What was he thinking! Tansy seemed so happy and relieved the last three days, that would surely be the wrong course to take.

But how could Tansy have got over a serious obsession so easily? It wasn't normal. He remembered her sleeping smile. Yet it wasn't Tansy who was behaving strangely now. It was he. As if a spell—What asinine rot! He'd just let himself be irritated by that stupid, hidebound old bunch of women, those old dragons—

His eyes instantly strayed toward the window, but the telephone recalled him.

"Professor Saylor? . . . I'm calling for Doctor Pollard. Could you come in and see Dr. Pollard this afternoon? . . . Four o'clock? Thank you."

He leaned back with a smile. At least, he told himself, he had got the chairmanship.

It grew darker as the day progressed, the ragged clouds swept lower and lower. Students scurried along the walks. But the storm held off until almost four.

Big raindrops splattered the dusty steps as he ducked under

the portico of the Administration Building. Thunder crackled and crashed, as if acres of metal sheeting were being shaken above the clouds. He turned back to watch. Lightning threw the Gothic roofs and towers into sharp relief. Again the crackle, building to a crash. He remembered he had left a window open in his office. But there was nothing that would be damaged by the wet.

Wind swooped through the portico with a strident, pulsating roar. The unmusical voice that spoke into his ear had the same quality.

"Isn't it a pretty storm?"

Evelyn Sawtelle was smiling for once. It had a grotesque effect on her features, as if a horse had suddenly discovered how to smirk.

"You've heard the news, of course?" She went on. "About Hervey."

Hervey popped out from behind her. He was grinning too, but embarrassedly. He mumbled something that was lost in the storm and extended his hand blindly, as if he were in a receiving line.

Evelyn never took her eyes off Norman. "Isn't it wonderful?" she said. "Of course, we expected it, but still—"

Norman guessed. He forced himself to grasp Hervey's hand, just as the latter was withdrawing it flusteredly.

"Congratulations, old man," he said briefly.

"I'm very proud of Hervey," Evelyn announced possessively, as if he were a small boy who had won a prize for good behavior.

Her eyes followed Norman's hand. "Oh, you've cut yourself." The smirk seemed to be a permanent addition to her features. The wind wailed fiendishly. "Come, Hervey!" And she walked out into the storm as if it weren't there.

Hervey goggled at her in surprise. He mumbled something apologetic to Norman, pumped his hand up and down again, and then obediently scampered after his wife.

Norman watched them. There was something unpleasantly impressive about the way Evelyn Sawtelle marched

through the sheets of rain, getting both of them drenched to
no purpose except to satisfy some strange obstinacy. He
could see that Hervey was trying to hurry her and not suc-
ceeding. Lightning flared viciously, but there was no reaction apparent in her angular, awkward frame. Once again
Norman became dimly aware of an alien, explosive emotion
deep within him.

And so that little poodle dog of hers, he thought, is to have
the final say on the educational policy of the sociology
department. Then what the devil does Pollard want to see me
for? To offer his commiserations?

Almost an hour later he slammed out of Pollard's office,
tense with anger, wondering why he had not handed in his
resignation on the spot. To be interrogated about his actions
like some kid, on the obvious instigation of busy-bodies like
Thompson and Mrs. Carr and Gracine Pollard! To have to
listen to a lot of hogwash about his "attitudes" and "the
Hempnell spirit," with veiled insinuations about his "moral
code."

At least he had given somewhat better than he had taken!
At least he had forced a note of confusion into that suave,
oratorical voice, and made those tufted gray eyebrows pop up
and down more than once!

He had to pass the Dean of Men's office. Mrs. Gunnison
was standing at the door. Like a big, oozy, tough-skinned
slug, he told himself, noting her twisted stockings and handbag stuffed full as a grab bag, the inevitable camera dangling
beside it. His exasperation shifted to her.

"Yes, I cut myself!" he told her, observing the direction
of her glance. His voice was hoarse from the tirade he had
delivered to Pollard.

Then he remembered something and did not stop to weigh
his words. "Mrs. Gunnison, you picked up my wife's diary
last night . . . by mistake. Will you please give it to me?"

"*You're* mistaken," she replied tolerantly.

"I saw you coming out of her bedroom with it."

Her eyes became lazy slits. "In that case you'd have

mentioned it last night. You're overwrought, Norman. I understand." She nodded toward Pollard's office. "It must have been quite a disappointment."

"I'm asking you to return the diary!"

"And you'd really better look after that cut," she continued unruffledly. "It doesn't look any too well bandaged, and it seems to be bleeding. Infections can be nasty things."

He turned on his heel and walked away. Her reflection confronted him, murky and dim in the glass of the outer door. She was smiling.

Outside, Norman looked at his hand. Evidently he had opened the cut when he banged Pollard's desk. He drew the bandage tighter.

The storm had blown over. Yellow sunlight was flooding from under the low curtain of clouds to the west, flashing richly from the wet roofs and upper windows. Surplus rain was sprinkling from the trees. The campus was empty. A flurry of laughter from the girls' dormitories etched itself, a light, harmless acid, on the silence. He shrugged aside his anger and let his senses absorb the new-washed beauty of the scene.

He prided himself on being able to enjoy the moment at hand. It seemed to him one of the chief signs of maturity.

He tried to think like a painter, identifying hues and shades, searching for the faint rose or green hidden in the shadows. There was really something to be said for Gothic architecture. Even though it was not functional, it carried the eye along pleasantly from one fanciful bit of stonework to the next. Now take those leafy finials topping the Estrey tower—

And then suddenly the sunlight was colder than ice, the roofs of Hempnell were like the roofs of hell, and the faint laughter like the crystalline cachinnations of fiends. Before he knew it, he had swerved sharply away from Morton, off the path and onto the wet grass, although he was only halfway across campus.

No need to go back to the office, he told himself shakily. Just a long climb for a few notes. They could wait until tomorrow. And why not go home a different way tonight? Why always take the direct route that led through the gate between Estrey and Morton, under those dark, overhanging ledges. Why—

He forced himself to look up again at the open window of his office. It was empty now, as he might have expected. That other thing must have been some moving blur in his vision, and imagination had done the rest, as when a small shadow scurrying across the floor becomes a spider.

Or perhaps a shade flapping outward—

But a shadow could hardly crawl along the ledge outside the windows. A blur could hardly move so slowly or retain such a definite form.

And then the way the thing had waited, peering in, before it dropped down inside. Like . . . Like a—

Of course it was all nonsense. And there really was no need whatsoever to bother about fetching those notes or closing the window. It would be giving in to a momentary fear. There was a rumble of distant thunder.

—Like a very large lizard, the color and texture of stone.

CHAPTER VIII

"—And henceforth his soul is believed to be knit up in a manner with the stone. If it breaks, it is an evil omen for him; they say that thunder has struck the stone and that he who owns it will soon die—"

No use. His eyes kept wandering over the mass of print. He laid the volume of *The Golden Bough* aside and leaned back. From somewhere to the east, the thunder still throbbed faintly. But the familiar leather of the easy-chair imparted a sense of security and detachment.

Suppose, just as an intellectual exercise, he tried to analyze the misfortunes and fancies of the past three days in terms of sorcery.

The cement dragon would be a clear case of sympathetic magic. Mrs. Gunnison animated it by means of her photographs—the old business of doing things to the image instead of the object, like sticking pins in a wax doll. Perhaps she had joined a number of photographs together to make a *motion* picture. Or perhaps she had managed to get a picture of the inside of his office and had clipped a picture of the dragon to it. Murmuring suitable incantations, of course. Or,

more simply, she might have slipped a picture of the dragon
into one of his pockets. He started to feel through them, then
reminded himself that this was only an intellectual exercise, a
trifling diversion for a tired brain.

But carry through on it. You've exhausted Mrs. Gunnison.
How about Evelyn Sawtelle? Her recording of the bull-
roarer, notable storm-summoner, would provide a neat magical explanation for the wind last night and the storm and
wind today—both associated with the Sawtelles. And then
the similar sound in his dream—he wrinkled his nose in
distaste.

He could hear Tansy calling Totem from the back porch,
rattling her little tin pan.

Put today's self-injurious acts in another category. The
obsidian knife. The razor blade. The cranky saucepan. The
carpet tack. The match that he had let burn his fingers a few
minutes ago.

Perhaps the razor blade had been charmed, like the en-
chanted sword or ax which wounds the person who wields it.
Perhaps someone had stolen the blood-smeared obsidian
knife and dropped it in water, so the wound would keep
flowing. That was a well-established superstition.

A dog was trotting along the sidewalk out in front. He
could distinctly hear the clop-clop of paws.

Tansy was still calling Totem.

Perhaps a sorcerer had commanded him to destroy himself
by inches—or millimeters, considering the razor blade. That
would explain all the self-injurious acts at one swoop. The
flat voice in the dream had ordered him to do it.

The dog had turned up the drive. His claws made a grating
sound on the concrete.

The tarot-card diagrams scribbled by Mrs. Sawtelle would
figure as some magical control mechanism. The stick-figure
of the man and the truck had grim implications if interpreted
in the light of his old irrational fear.

It really didn't sound so much like a dog. Probably the
neighbor's boy dragging home by jerks some indeterminate

bulky object. The neighbor's boy devoted all his spare time to collecting trash.

"Totem! Totem!" Followed by, "All right, stay out if you want to," and the sound of the back door closing.

Finally, that very trite "sense of a presence" just behind him. Taller than himself, hands poised to grab. Only whenever he looked over his shoulder, it dodged. Something resembling it had figured in the dream—the source, perhaps, of that flat voice. And in that case—

His patience snapped. An intellectual exercise all right! For morons! He stubbed out his cigarette.

"Well, I've done my duty. That cat can sing for her supper." Tansy sat on the arm of the chair and put her hand on Norman's shoulder. "How are things going?"

"Not so good," he replied lightly.

"The chairmanship?"

He nodded. "Sawtelle got it."

Tansy cursed fluently. It did him good to hear her.

"Make you want to take up conjuring again?" He bit his lip. He certainly hadn't intended to say that.

She looked at him closely.

"What do you mean by that?" she asked.

"Just a joke."

"Are you sure? I know you've been worrying about me these last few days, ever since you found out. Wondering if I were going totally neurotic on you, and watching for the next symptoms. Now, dear, you don't have to deny it. It was the natural thing. I expected you'd be suspicious of me for a while. With your knowledge of psychiatry, it would be impossible for you to believe that anyone could shake off an obsession so quickly. And I've been so happy to get free from all that, that your suspicions haven't bothered me. I've known they would wear off."

"But, darling, I honestly haven't been suspicious," he protested. "Maybe I ought to have been, but I haven't."

Her gray-green eyes were sphinxlike. She said slowly, "Then what are you worrying about?"

"Nothing at all." Here was where he had to be very careful.

She shook her head. "That's not true. You are worrying. Oh, I know there are some things on your mind that you haven't told me about. It isn't that."

He looked up quickly.

She nodded. "About the chairmanship. And about some student who's been threatening you. And about that Van Nice girl. You didn't really think, did you, that Hempnell would let me miss those delightful scandals?" She smiled briefly as he started to protest. "Oh, I know you aren't the type who seduces love-struck mimeograph operators, not neurotic ones at any rate." She became serious again. "Those are all minor matters, things you can take in your stride. You didn't tell me about them because you were afraid I might backslide from the desire to protect you. Isn't that right?"

"Yes."

"But I have the feeling that what you're worrying about goes much deeper than that. Yesterday and today I've even felt that you wanted to turn to me for help, and didn't dare."

He paused, as if thinking exactly how to phrase his answer. But he was studying her face, trying to read the exact meaning of each familiar quirk of expression around the mouth and eyes. She looked very contained, but that was only a mask, he thought. Actually, in spite of everything she said, she must still be poised close to the brink of her obsession. One little push, such as a few careless words on his part—How the devil had he ever let himself get so enmeshed in his own worries and those ridiculous projections of his cranky imagination? Here a few inches away from him was the only thing that mattered—the mind behind this smooth forehead and these clear, gray-green eyes; to steer that mind away from any such ridiculous notions as those he had been indulging in, the last few days.

"To tell the truth," he siad, "I *have* been worried about you. I thought it would hurt your self-confidence if I let you know. Maybe I was unwise—you seem to have sensed it, anyway—but that's what I thought. The way you feel now, of course, it can't possibly hurt you to know.''

It occurred to him that it was almost frighteningly easy to lie convincingly to someone you loved.

She did not give in at once. ''Are you sure?'' she asked. ''I still have the feeling there's more to it.''

Suddenly she smiled and yielded to the pressure of his arms. ''It must be the MacKnight in me—my Scotch ancestry,'' she said, laughing. ''Awfully stubborn, you know. Monomaniacs. When we're crazy on a thing, we're completely crazy, but when we drop it, we drop it all at once. Like my great-uncle Peter. You know, the one who left the Presbyterian ministry and gave up Christianity on the very same day he proved to his satisfaction there was no God. Remember, at the age of seventy-two?'' There was a long and grumbling roll of thunder.

The storm was coming back.

''Well, I'm very glad you're only worried about me,'' she continued. ''It's complimentary, and I like it.''

She was smiling happily, but there was still something enigmatic about the eyes, something withheld. As he was congratulating himself on carrying it off successfully, it suddenly occurred to him that two could play at the game of lying. She might be holding something back herself, with the idea of reassuring him. She might be trying to protect him from her own blacker worries. Her subtlety might undercut his own. No sane reason to suspect that, and yet—

''Suppose I get us a drink,'' she said, ''and we decide whether or not you leave Hempnell this year, and look for greener fields.''

He nodded. She started around the bend in the L-shaped room.

—And yet, you could live with and love a person for fifteen years, and not know what was behind her eyes.

There was the rattle of glassware from the sideboard, and the friendly sound of a full bottle set down.

Then, timed to the thunder, but much closer, a shuddering, animal scream. It was cut off before Norman had sprung to his feet.

As he cleared the angle of the room, he saw Tansy going through the kitchen door. She was a little ahead of him down the back steps.

Light fanned out from the windows of the opposite house into the service yard. It revealed the sprawled body of Totem, head mashed flat against the concrete.

He heard a little sound start and stop in Tansy's throat. It might have been a gasp, or a sob, or a snarl.

The light revealed little more than the body. Norman moved so that his feet covered the two prominent scuffs in the concrete just beyond the body. They might have been caused by the impact of a brick or heavy stone, perhaps the thing that had killed Totem, but there was something so suggestive about their relative position that he did not want Tansy's imagination to have a chance to work on them.

She lifted her face. It didn't show much emotion.

"You'd better go in," he said.

"You'll—"

He nodded. "Yes."

She stopped halfway up the stairs. "That was a rotten, rotten thing for anybody to do."

"Yes."

She left the door open. A moment later she came out and laid on the porch railing a square of heavy cloth, covered with shed hair. Then she went in again and shut the door.

He rolled up the cat's body and stopped at the garage for the spade. He did not spend time searching for any brick or heavy stone or other missile. Nor did he examine closer the heavy footmarks he fancied he saw in the grass beyond the service yard.

Lightning began to flicker as his space bit into the soft ground by the back fence. He kept his mind strictly on the task at hand. He worked steadily, but without undue haste. When he patted down the last spadeful of earth and started for the house, the lightning flashes were stronger, making the moments in between even darker. A wind started up and dragged at the leaves.

He did not hurry. What if the lighting did indistinctly show him a large dog near the front of the house? There were several large dogs in the neighborhood. They were not savage. Totem had not been killed by a dog.

Deliberately he replaced the spade in the garage and walked back to the house. Only when he got inside and looked back through the screen did his thoughts break loose for a moment.

The lightning flash, brightest yet, showed the dog coming around the corner of the house. He had only a glimpse. A dog the color of concrete. It walked stiff-legged. He quickly closed the door and shot home the bolt.

Then he remembered that the study windows were open. He must close them. Quickly.

It might rain in.

CHAPTER IX

WHEN NORMAN ENTERED the living room his face was outwardly serene. Tansy was sitting on the straight chair, leaning a little forward, an intent moody expression around her
eyes. Her hands were playing absently with a bit of twine.

He carefully lit a cigarette.

"Do you want that drink now?" he asked, not too casually, not too sharply.

"No, thanks. You have one." Her hands kept on knotting
and unknotting the twine.

He sat down and picked up his book. From the easy-chair
he could watch her unobtrusively.

And now that he had no grave to dig or other mechanical
task to perform, his thoughts were not to be denied. But at
least he could keep them circling in a little isolated sphere
inside his skull, without affecting either the expression of his
face or the direction of his other thoughts, which were protec-
tively concentrated on Tansy.

"Sorcery *is*," went the thoughts inside the sphere.
"Something has been conjured down from a roof. Women
are witches fighting for their men. Tansy was a witch. She
was guarding you. But you made her stop."

"In that case," he replied swiftly to the thoughts inside the sphere, "why isn't Tansy aware of what's happening? It can't be denied that she has acted very relieved and happy."

"Are you sure she isn't aware or becoming aware?" answered the thoughts inside the sphere. "Besides, in losing her instruments of magic she probably lost her sensitivity to magic. Without *his* instruments—say microscope or telescope—a scientist would be no better able than a savage to see the germs of typhoid or the moons of Mars. His natural sensory equipment might even be inferior to that of the savage."

And the imprisoned thoughts buzzed violentely, like bees seeking escape from a stopped-up hive.

"Norman," Tansy said abruptly, without looking at him, "you found and burned that hand in your watch charm, didn't you?"

He thought a moment. "Yes, I did," he said lightly.

"I'd really forgotten about that. There were so many."

He turned a page, and then another. Thunder crackled loudly and rain began to patter on the roof.

"Norman, you burned the diary, too, didn't you? You were right in doing it, of course. I held it back, because it didn't contain actual spells already laid, only the formulas for them. So in a twisted illogical way I pretended it didn't count. But you did burn it?"

That was harder to answer. He felt as if he were playing a guessing game and Tansy were getting perilously "warm." The thoughts in the sphere buzzed triumphantly: "Mrs. Gunnison has the diary. Now she knows all of Tansy's protective charms."

But he lied, "Yes, I burnt it. I'm sorry, but I thought—"

"Of course," Tansy cut in. "You were quite right." Her fingers played more rapidly with the cord. She did not look down at it.

Lightning showed flashes of pale street and trees through the window. The patter of rain became a pelting. But through it he fancied he heard the scrunch of paws on the drive.

Ridiculous—rain and wind were making too much noise.

His eyes were attracted by the pattern of the knots Tansy's restless fingers were weaving. They were complicated, strong-looking knots which fell apart at a single cunning jerk, reminding him of how Tansy had studied assiduously the cat's cradles of the Indians. It also recalled to his mind how knots are used by primitive people, to tie and loose the winds, to hold loved ones, to noose far-off enemies, to inhibit or free all manner of physical and physiological processes. And how the Fates weave destinies like threads. He found something very pleasing in the pattern of the knots and the rhythmic movements which produced them. They seemed to signify security. Until they fell apart.

"Norman,"—the voice was preoccupied and rapid—"what was that snapshot you asked Hulda Gunnison to show you last night?"

He felt a brief flurry of panic. She was getting "very warm." This was the stage of the game where you cried out "Hot!"

And then he heard the heavy, unyielding clump-clump of the boards of the front porch, seeming to move questioningly along the wall. The sphere of alien thoughts began to exert an irresistible centrifugal pressure. He felt his sanity being smothered between the assaults from within and without. Very deliberately he shaved off the ash of his cigarette against the edge of the tray.

"It was a picture of the roof of Estrey," he said casually. "Gunnison told me Hulda had taken a number of pictures of that sort. I wanted to see a sample."

"Some sort of creature in it, wasn't there?" Knots flickered into being and vanished with bewildering speed. It seemed to him suddenly that more than twine was being manipulated, and more than empty air tied and loosed. As if the knots were somehow creating an influence, as an electric current along a twisted wire creates a complex magnetic field.

"No," he said, and then made himself chuckle, "unless

you count in a stray cement dragon or two.'' He watched the rippling twine. At times it seemed to glitter, as if there were a metal strand in it.

If ordinary cords and knots, magically employed, could control winds, what would a part-metal cord control? Lightning?

Thunder ripped and crashed deafeningly. Lightning might have struck in the neighborhood. Tansy did not move a muscle. "That was a Lulu," Norman started to say. Then, as the thunder crash trailed off in rumblings and there was a second's lull in the rain, he heard the sound of something leaping heavily down from the front porch toward the large low window, behind him.

He got to his feet and managed to take a few steps toward the window, as if to look out at the storm. As he passed Tansy's chair he saw that her rippling fingers were creating a strange knot resembling a flower, with seven loops for petals. She stared like a sleep walker. Then he was between her and the window, shielding her.

The next lightning flash showed him what he knew he must see. It crouched, facing the window. The head was still blank and crude as an unfinished skull.

In the ensuing surge of blackness, the sphere of alien thoughts expanded with instant swiftness, until it occupied his entire mind.

He glanced behind him. Tansy's hands were still. The strange seven-looped knot was poised between them.

Just as he was turning back, he saw the hands jerk apart and the loops whip in like a seven-fold snare—and hold.

And in that same moment of turning he saw the street brighten like day and a great ribbon of lightning split the tall elm opposite and fork into several streams which streaked across the street toward the window and the stony form upreared against it.

Then—blinding light, and a tingling electrical surge through his whole body.

But on his retina was burned the incandescent track of the

lightning, whose multiple streams, racing toward the up-reared stony form, had converged upon it as if drawn together by a seven-fold knot.

The sphere of alien thoughts expanded beyond his skull at a dizzy rate, vanished.

His gasping, uncontrollable laughter rose above the dying reverberations of the titanic thunder blast. He dragged open the window, pulled a bridge lamp up to it, jerked the cover from the lamp so its light flooded outward.

"Look, Tansy!" he called, his words mixed with the manic laughter. "Look what those crazy students have done! Those frat men, I bet, I kidded in class. Look what they dragged down from campus and stuck in our front yard. Of all the crazy things—we'll have to call Buildings and Grounds to take it away tomorrow."

Rain splattered in his face. There was a sulphurous, metallic odor. Her hand touched his shoulder. She stared out blankly, her eyes still asleep.

It stood there, propped against the wall, solid and inert as only the inorganic can be. In some places the cement was darkened and fused.

"And of all mad coincidences," he gasped, "the lightning had to go and strike it."

On an impulse, he reached out his hand and touched it. At the feel of the rough, unyielding surface, still hot from the lightning flash, his laughter died.

"*Eppur si muove*," he murmured to himself, so low that even Tansy, standing beside him, might not have heard. "*Eppur si muove*."

CHAPTER X

NEXT DAY THE APPEARANCE Norman presented to Hempnell was a close approximation of that of a soldier suffering from battle-fatigue. He had had a long and heavy sleep, but he looked as if he were stupefied by weariness and nervous strain. And he was. Even Harold Gunnison remarked on it.

"It's nothing," Norman replied. "I'm just lazy."

Gunnison smiled skeptically. "You've been working too hard. It butchers efficiency. Better ration your hours of work. You jobs won't go hungry if you feed them eight hours a day.

"Trustees are queer cusses," he continued with apparent irrelevance. "And in some ways Pollard is more of a politician than an educator. But he brings in the money, and that's what college presidents are for."

Norman was grateful for Gunnison's tactful commiseration on his loss of the sociology chairmanship, especially since he knew it cost Harold an effort to criticize Pollard in any way. But he felt as far removed from Gunnison as from the hordes of gaily dressed students who filled the walks and socialized in clusters. As if there were a wall of faintly clouded glass between him and them. His only aim—and

even that was blurred—was to prolong his present state of
fatigued reaction from last night's events and to avoid all
thoughts.

Thoughts are dangerous, he told himself, and thoughts
against all science, all sanity, all civilized intelligence, are
the most dangerous of all. He felt their presence here and
there in his brain, like pockets of poison, harmless as long as
you left them encysted and did not prick them.

One was more familiar than the others. It had been there
last night at the height of the storm. He felt vaguely thankful
that he could no longer see inside of it.

Another thought-cyst was concerned with Tansy, and why
she had seemed so cheerful and forgetful this morning.

Another—a very large one—was sunk so deeply in his
mind that he could only perceive a small section of its
globular surface. He knew it was connected with an unfamiliar, angry, destructive emotion that he had yesterday sensed
in himself more than once, and he knew that it must under no
circumstances be disturbed. He could feel it pulsate slowly
and rhythmically, like a monster asleep in mud.

Another had to do with hands—hands in flannel gloves.

Another—tiny but prominent—was somehow concerned
with cards.

And there were more, many more.

His situation was akin to that of the legendary hero who
must travel through a long and narrow corridor, without once
touching the morbidly enticing, poisoned walls.

He knew he could not avoid contact with the thought-cysts
indefinitely, but in the meantime they might shrink and
disappear.

The day fitted his superficially dull and lethargic mood.
Instead of the cool spell that should have followed the storm,
there was a foretaste of summer in the air. Student absences
rose sharply. Those who came to class were inattentive and
exhibited other symptoms of spring fever.

Only Bronstein seemed animated. He kept drawing Norman's other students aside by twos and threes, and whisper-

ing to them animatedly, heatedly. Norman found out that he was trying to get up a petition of protest on Sawtelle's appointment. Norman asked him to stop it. Bronstein refused, but in any case he seemed to be failing in the job of arousing the other students.

Norman's lectures were languid. He contented himself with transforming his notes into accurate verbal statements with a minimum of mental effort. He watched the pencils move methodically as notes were taken, or wander off into intricate doodles. Two girls were engrossed in sketching the handsome profile of the fraternity president in the second row. He watched foreheads wrinkle as they picked up the thread of his lecture, smooth out again as they dropped it.

And all the while his own mind was wandering off on side tracks too dreamlike and irrational to be called thoughts. They consisted of mere trails of words, like a psychologist's association test.

One such trail began when he recalled the epigram about a lecture being a process of transferring the contents of the teacher's notebook into the notebooks of the students, without allowing it to pass through the minds of either. That made him think of mimeographing.

Mimeograph, it went on. Margaret Van Nice. Theodore Jennings. Gun. Windowpane. Galileo. Scroll—(Sheer away from that! Forbidden territory.)

The daydream backtracked and took a different turning. Jennings. Gunnison. Pollard. President. Emperor. Empress. Juggler. Tower. Hanged Man—(Hold on! Don't go any further.)

As the long dull day wore on, the daydreams gradually assumed a uniform coloration.

Gun. Knife. Sliver. Broken glass. Nail. Tetanus.

After his last class he retreated to his office and moped and fussed around on little jobs, so preoccupied that at times he forgot what he was doing. The daydreams still wouldn't let him alone.

War. Mangled bodies. Mayhem. Murder. Rope.

Hangman. (Sheer off again!) Gas. Gun. Poison.

The coloration of blood and physical injury.

And ever more strongly he felt the slow-pulsing respiration of the monster in the depths of his mind, dreaming nightmares of carnage from which it would soon awaken and heave up out of the mud. And he powerless to stop it. It was as if a crusted-over swamp, swollen with underground water, were pushing up the seemingly healthy ground by imperceptible degrees—nearing the point when it would burst through in one vast slimy eruption.

Starting home, Norman fell in with Mr. Carr.

"Good evening, Norman," said the old gentleman, lifting his Panama hat to mop his forehead, which merged into an extensive bald area.

"Good evening, Linthicum," said Norman. But his mind was occupied with speculating how, if a man let a thumbnail grow and then sharpened it carefully, he could cut the veins of his wrist and so bleed to death.

Mr. Carr wiped the handkerchief under his beard.

"I enjoyed the bridge thoroughly," he said. "Perhaps the four of us could have a game when the ladies are away at the faculty wives' meeting next Thursday? You and I could be partners and use the Culbertson slam conventions." His voice became wistful. "I'm tired of always having to play the Blackwood."

Norman nodded, but he was thinking of how men have learned to swallow their tongues, when the occasion came, and die of suffocation. He tried to check himself. These were speculations appropriate only to the concentration camp. Visions of death kept rising in his mind, replacing one another. He felt the pulsations of the thing below his thoughts become almost unendurably strong. Mr. Carr nodded pleasantly and turned off. Norman quickened his pace, as if the walls of the poisoned passageway were contracting on the legendary hero and, unless the end were soon reached, he would have to shove out against them wildly.

From the corner of his eye he saw one of his students. She

was staring puzzedly, at him, or at something behind him. He brushed past her.

He reached the boulevard. The lights were against him. He paused on the curb. A large red truck was rumbling toward the intersection at a fair rate of speed.

And then he knew just what was going to happen, and that he would be unable to stop himself.

He was going to wait until the truck was very close and then he was going to throw himself under the wheels. End of the passageway.

That was the meaning of the fifth stick figure, the tarot diagram that had departed from tradition.

Empress—Juggler—The truck was very close. Tower—The light had started to change but the truck was not going to stop. Hanged man—

It was only when he leaned forward, tensing his leg muscles, that the small flat voice spoke into his ear, a voice that was a monotone and yet diabolically humorous, the voice of his dreams:

"Not for two weeks, at least. Not for two more weeks."

He regained his balance. The truck thundered by. He looked over his shoulder—first up, then around. No one but a small Negro boy and an elderly man, rather shabbily dressed, carrying a shopping bag. Neither of them near him. A shiver settled on his spine.

Hallucinations, of course, he told himself. That voice had been inside his head. Nevertheless his eyes shifted warily from side to side, probing the very air for hints of the unseen, as he crossed the street and proceeded home. As soon as he was inside, he poured himself a more than generous drink. Oddly, Tansy had set out soda and whiskey on the sideboard. He mixed the highball and gulped it down. Mixed himself another, took a gulp, then looked at the glass doubtfully.

Just then he heard a car stop and a moment later Tansy came in, carrying a bundle. Her face was smiling and a little flushed. With a sigh of relief she set down the bundle and pushed aside the dark bangs from her forehead.

"Whew! What a muggy day. I thought you'd be wanting a drink. Here, let me finish that one for you."

When she put down the glass there was only ice in it, "There, now we're blood brothers or something. Mix yourself another."

"That was my second," he told her.

"Oh, heck, I thought I was cheating you." She sat on the edge of the table and wagged a finger in his face. "Look, mister, you need a rest. Or some excitement. I'm not sure which. Maybe both. Now here's my plan. I make us a cold supper—sandwiches. Then, when it's dark we get in Oscar and drive to the Hill. We haven't done that for years. How about it, mister?"

He hesitated. Helped by the drink, his thoughts were veering. Half his mind was still agonizing over the hallucination he'd just experienced, with its unnerving suggestion of unsuspected suicidal impulses and . . . he wasn't sure what. The other half was coming under the spell of Tansy's gaiety.

She reached and pinched his nose. "How about it?"

"All right," he said.

"Hey, you're supposed to act interested!" She slid off the table, started for the kitchen, then added darkly over her shoulder, "But that will come later."

She looked provocatively pretty. He couldn't see any difference between now and fifteen years ago. He felt he was seeing her for the hundredth first time.

Feeling halfway relaxed at last, or at least diverted, he sat down in the easy chair. But as he did, he felt something hard and angular indent his thigh. He stood up quickly, stuck his hand in his trousers pocket, and drew out Theodore Jennings' revolver.

He stared at it frightenedly, unable to recall when he had taken it from the drawer at the office. Then, with a quick glance toward the kitchen, he hurried over to the sideboard, opened the bottom drawer, stuffed it under a pile of linen.

When the sandwiches came, he was reading the evening paper. He had just found a local-interest item at the bottom of the fifth page.

A practical joke is worth any amount of trouble and physical exertion. At least, that is the sentiment of a group of Hempnell College students, as yet unidentified. But we are wondering about the sentiments of Professor Norman Saylor, when he looked out the window this morning and saw a stone gargoyle weighing a good three hundred pounds sitting in the middle of his lawn. It had been removed from the roof of one of the college buildings. How the students managed to detach it, lower it from the roof, and transport it to Professor Saylor's residence, is still a mystery.

When President Randolph Pollard was asked about the pranksters, he laughingly replied, "I guess our physical education program must be providing our men with exceptional reserves of strength and energy."

When we spoke to President Pollard he was leaving to address the Lions' Club on "The Greater Hempnell: College and Town." (For details of his address, see Page 1.)

Just what you might expect. The usual inaccuracies. It wasn't a gargoyle; gargoyles are ornamental rainspouts. And then no mention at all of the lightning. Probably the reporter had suppressed it because it didn't fit into any of the convention patterns for supposedly unconventional news stories. Newspapers were supposed to love coincidences, but God, the weird ones they missed!

Finally, the familiar touch of turning the item into an advertisement for the physical-education department. You had to admit that the Hempnell publicity office had a kind of heavy-handed efficiency.

Tansy swept the paper out of his hands.

"The world can wait," she said. "Here, have a bite of my sandwich."

CHAPTER XI

IT WAS QUITE DARK when they started for the Hill. Norman drove carefully, taking his time at intersections. Tansy's gaiety still did no more than hold in check the other half of his thoughts.

She was smiling mysteriously. She had changed to a white sports dress. She looked like one of his students.

"I might be a witch," she said, "taking you to a hilltop rendezvous. Our own private Sabbat."

Norman started. Then he quickly reminded himself that when she said things like that, she was making a courageous mockery of her previous behavior. He must on no account let her see the other half of his thoughts.

It would never do to let her realize how badly worried he was about himself.

The lights of the town dropped behind. Half a mile out, he turned off sharply onto the road that wound up the Hill. It was bumpier than he remembered from the last time—was it as much as ten years ago? And the trees were thicker, their twigs brushing the windshield.

When they emerged into the half acre of clearing on the top, the red moon, two days after full, was rising.

Tansy pointed to it and said, "Check! I timed it perfectly.
But where are the others? There always used to be two or
three cars up here. And on a night like this!"

He stopped the car close to the edge. "Fashions in lovers'
lanes change like anything else," he told her. "We're traveling a disused folkway."

"Always the sociologist!"

"I guess so. Maybe Mrs. Carr found out about this place.
And I suppose the students range farther afield nowadays."

She rested her head on his shoulder. He switched off the
headlights, and the moon cast soft shadows.

"We used to do this at Gorham," Tansy murmured.
"When I was taking your classes, and you were the serious
young instructor. Until I found out you weren't any different
from the college boys—only better. Remember?"

He nodded and took her hand. He looked down at the
town, made out the campus, with its prominent floodlights
designed to chase couples out of dark corners. Those garishly
floodlighted Gothic buildings seemed for the moment to
symbolize a whole world of barren intellectual competition
and jealous traditionalism, a world which at the moment he
felt to be infinitely alien.

"I wonder if this is why they hate us so?" he asked, almost
without thinking.

"Whatever are you talking about?" But the question
sounded lazy.

"I mean the rest of the faculty, or most of them. Is it
because we can do things like this?"

She laughed. "So you're actually coming alive. We don't
do things like this so very often, you know."

He kept on with his idea. "It's a devilishly competitive
and jealous world. And competition in an institution can be
nastier than any other kind, because it's so confined. Think
so?"

"I've lived with it for years," said Tansy simply.

"Of course, it's all very petty. But petty feelings can come
to outweigh big ones. Their size is better suited to the human
mind."

He looked down at Hempnell and tried to visualize the amount of ill will and jealousy he had inevitably accumulated for himself. He felt a slight chill creeping on his skin. He realized where this train of thought was leading. The darker half of his mind loomed up.

"Here, philosopher," said Tansy, "have a slug."

She was offering him a small silver flask.

He recognized it. "I never dreamed you'd kept it all these years."

"Uh-huh. Remember when I first offered you a drink from it? You were a trifle shocked, I believe."

"I took the drink."

"Uh-huh. So take this one."

It tasted like fire and spice. There were memories in it, too, memories of those crazy prohibition years, and of Gorham and New England.

"Brandy?"

"Greek. Give me some."

The memories flooded over the darker half of his mind. It disappeared beneath their waves. He looked at Tansy's sleek hair and moon-glowing eyes. Of course she's a witch, he thought lightly. She's Lilith. Ishtar. He'd tell her so.

"Do you remember the time," he said, "we slid down the bank to get away from the night watchman at Gorham? There would have been a magnificent scandal if he'd caught us."

"Oh, yes, and the time—"

When they went down the hill, the moon was an hour higher. He drove slowly. No need to imitate the sillier practices of the prohibition era. A truck chugged past him. "Two more weeks." Rot! Who'd he think he was, hearing voices? Joan of Arc?

He felt hilarious. He wanted to tell Tansy all the ridiculous things he'd been imagining the last few days, so she could laugh at them, too. It would make a swell ghost story. There was a reason he shouldn't tell her, but now it seemed an insignificant reason—part and parcel of this cramped, warped, overcautious Hempnell life they ought to break away from more often. What was life worth, anyway, if you had to sit around remembering not to mention this, that, and the other thing because someone else might be upset?

So when they arrived in the living room and Tansy flopped down on the sofa, he began, "You know, Tansy, about this witch stuff. I want to tell you—"

He was caught completely off guard by whatever force, real or unreal, hit him. A moment later he was sitting in the easy chair, completely sober, with the outer world an ice pressure on his senses, the inner world a whirling sphere of alien thought, and the future a dark corridor two weeks long.

It was as if a very large, horny hand had been clapped roughly over his mouth, and as if another such hand had grasped him by the shoulder, shaken him, and slammed him down in the leather chair.

As if?

He looked around uneasily.

Maybe there had been hands.

Apparently Tansy had not noticed anything. Her face was a white oval in the gloom. She was still humming a snatch of song. She did not ask what he had started to say.

He got up, walked unsteadily into the dining room, and poured himself a drink from the sideboard. On the way he switched on the lights.

So he couldn't tell Tansy or anyone else about it, even if he wanted to? That was why you never heard from real witch-craft victims, he told himself, his thoughts for the moment quite out of hand. And why they never seemed able to escape, even if the means of escape were at hand. It wasn't weak will. They were *watched*. Like a gangster taken on a ride from an expensive night-club. He must excuse himself from the loud-mouthed crowd at his table and laugh heartily, and stop to chat with friends and throw a wink at the pretty girls, because right behind him are those white-scarfed trigger boys, hands in the pockets of their velvet-collared dress overcoats. No use dying now. Better play along. There might be a chance.

But that was thriller stuff, movie stuff.

So were the horny hands.

He nodded at himself in the glass above the sideboard.

"Meet Professor Saylor," he said, "the distinguished ethnologist and firm believer in real witchcraft."

But the face in the glass did not look so much disgusted as frightened.

He mixed himself another drink, and one for Tansy, and took them into the living room.

"Here's to wickedness," said Tansy. "Do you realize that you haven't been anywhere near drunk since Christmas?"

He grinned. Getting drunk was just what the movie gangster would do, to grab a moment of forgetfulness when the Big Boy had put him on the spot. And not a bad idea.

Slowly, and at first only in a melancholy minor key, the mood of the Hill returned. They talked, played old records, told jokes that were old enough to be young again. Tansy hammered at the piano and they sang a crazy assortment of songs, folk songs, hymns, national anthems, workers' and revolutionists' songs, blues, Brahms, Schubert—haltingly at first, later at the top of their voices.

They remembered.

And they kept on drinking.

But always, like a shimmering sphere of crystal, the alien thoughts spun in Norman's mind. The drink made it possible for him to regard them dispassionately, without constant revulsions in the name of common sense. With the singlemindedness of inebriation, his scholar's mind began to assemble world-wide evidence of witchcraft.

For instance, was it not likely that all self-destructive impulses were the result of witchcraft? Those universal impulses that were a direct contradiction to the laws of self-preservation and survival. To account for them, Poe had fancifully conceived an "Imp of the Perverse," and psychoanalysts had laboriously hypothesized a "death wish." How much simpler to attribute them to malign forces outside the individual, working by means as yet unanalyzed and therefore classified as supernatural.

His experiences during the past days could be divided into two categories. The first included those natural misfortunes and antagonisms from which Tansy's magic had screened him. The attack on his life by Theodore Jennings should probably be placed in this category. The chances were that Jennings was actually psychopathic. He would have made his murderous attack at an earlier date, had not Tansy's magic kept it from getting started. As soon as her protective screen was down, as soon as Norman burned the last hand, the idea had suddenly burgeoned in Jennings' mind like a hothouse flower. Jennings had himself admitted it. "I didn't realize it until this minute—"

Margaret Van Nice's accusation, Thompson's sudden burst of interest in his extracurricular activities, and Saw-telle's chance discovery of the Cunningham thesis probably belong in the same category.

In the second category—active and malign witchcraft, directed against himself.

"A penny for your thoughts," offered Tansy, looking over the rim of her glass.

"I was thinking of the party last Christmas," he replied smoothly, though in a somewhat blurred voice, "and of how Welby crawled around playing a St. Bernard, with the bearskin rug over his shoulders and the bottle of whiskey slung under his neck. And I was wondering why the best fun always seems so trite afterward. But I'd rather be trite than respectable." He felt a childish pride in his cunning at having avoided being trapped into admission. He simultaneously thought of Tansy as a genuine witch and as a potentially neurotic individual who had to be protected at all costs from dangerous suggestions. The liquor made his mind work by parts, and the parts had no check on each other.

Things began to happen by fits and starts. His consciousness began to black out, though in the intervals between, his thoughts went on with an exaggerated scholarly solemnity.

They were wailing, "St. James Infirmary."

He was thinking: "Why shouldn't the women be the

witches? They're the intuitionalists, the traditionalists, the irrationalists. They're superstitious to start with. And like Tansy, most of them are probably never quite sure whether or not their witchcraft really works.''

They had shoved back the carpet and were dancing to ''Chloe.'' Sometime or other Tansy had changed to her rose dressing gown.

He was thinking: ''In the second category, put the Estrey dragon. Animated by a human or nonhuman soul conjured into it by Mrs. Gunnison and controlled through photographs. Put also the obsidian knife, the obedient wind, and the obdurate truck.''

They were playing a record of Ravel's ''Bolero,'' and he was beating out the rhythm with his fist.

He was thinking: ''Business men buy stocks on the advice of fortune-tellers, numerologists rule the careers of movie stars, half the world governs its actions by astrology, advertisements bleat constantly of magic and miracles, and most modern and all surrealist art is nothing but attempted witchcraft, borrowing its forms from the primitive witchdoctor and its ideas from the modern theosophist.''

He was watching Tansy as she sang ''St. Louis Blues'' in a hoarsely throbbing voice. It was true, just as Welby had always maintained, that she had a genuine theatrical flair. Make a good chanteuse.

He was thinking: ''Tansy stopped the Estrey dragon with the knots. But she'll have a hard time doing anything like that again because Mrs. Gunnison has her book of formulas and can figure out ways to circumvent her.''

They were sharing a highball that would have burned his throat if his throat had not been numb, and he seemed to be getting most of it.

He was thinking: ''The stick figure of the man and the truck is the key to a group of related sorceries. Cards began as instruments of magic, like art. These sorceries aim at finishing me off. The bull-roarer acts as an amplifier. The invisible thing standing behind me, with the flat voice and heavy hands, is a guardian, to see to it that I do not deviate from the path appointed. Narrow corridor. Two weeks more.''

The strange thing was that these thoughts were not altogether unpleasant. They had a wild, black, poisonous beauty of their own, a lovely, deadly shimmer. They possessed the fascination of the impossible, the incredible. They hinted at unimaginable vistas. Even while they terroized, they did not lose that chillingly poignant beauty. They were like the visions conjured up by some forbidden drug. They had the lure of an unknown sin and an ultimate blasphemy. Norman could understand the force that compelled the practitioners of black magic to take any risk.

His drunkenness made him feel safe. It had broken his mind down into its ultimate particles, and those particles were incapable of fear because they could not be injured. Just as the atoms in a man are not slain by the bullet that slays him.

But now the particles were whirling crazily. Consciousness was wavering.

He and Tansy were in each other's arms.

Tansy was asking eagerly, coaxingly, "All that's mine is yours? All that's yours is mine?"

The question awakened a suspicion in his mind, but he could not grasp it clearly. Something made him think that the words held a trap. But what trap? His thoughts stumbled.

She was saying—it sounded like the Bible—"And I have drunk from your cup and you have drunk from mine—''

Her face was a blurred oval, her eyes like misty jewels.

"Everything you have is mine? You give it to me without hindrance and of your own free choice?"

Somewhere a trap.

But the voice was irresistibly coaxing, like caressing fingers.

"All you have is mine? Just say it once, Norm, just once. For me.''

Of course he loved her. Better than anything in the world. He drew the blurred face toward him, tried to kiss the misty eyes.

"Yes . . . yes . . . everything—" he heard himself saying.

And then his mind toppled and plunged down into a fathomless ocean of darkness and silence and peace.

CHAPTER XII

SUNLIGHT MADE A BRIGHT, creamy design on the drawn blind. Filtered sunlight filled the bedroom, like a coolly glowing liquid. The birds were chirruping importantly. Norman closed his eyes again and stretched luxuriously.

Let's see, it was about time he got started on that article for *The American Anthropologist*. And there was still some work to do on the revision of his *Textbook of Ethnology*. Lots of time, but better get it out of the way. And he ought to have a serious talk with Bronstein about his thesis. That boy had some good ideas, but he needed a balance wheel. And then his address to the Off-campus Mothers. Might as well tell them something useful . . . .

Eyes still closed, he enjoyed that most pleasant of all sensations—the tug of work a man likes to do and is able to do well, yet that needn't be done immediately.

For today was certainly too good a day for golf to miss. Might see what Gunnison was doing. And then he and Tansy had not made an expedition into the country this whole spring. He'd talk to her about it, at breakfast. Saturday breakfast was an event. She must be getting it ready now. He felt as if a shower would make him very hungry. Must be late.

He opened one eye and focused on the bedroom clock. Twelve thirty-five? Say, just when had he got to bed last night? What had he been doing?

Memory of the past few days uncoiled like a spring, so swiftly that it started his heart pounding. Yet there was a difference now in his memories. From the very first moment they all seemed incredible and unreal. He had the sensation of reading the very detailed case-history of another person, a person with a lot of odd ideas about witchcraft, suicide, persecution, and what not else. His memories could not be made to fit with his present sense of well-being. What was stranger, they did not seriously disturb that sense of well-being.

He searched his mind diligently for traces of super-natural fear, of the sense of being watched and guarded, of that monstrous self-destructive impulse. He could not discover or even suggest to himself the slightest degree of such emotions. Whatever they had been, they were now part of the past, beyond the reach of everything except intellectual memory. "Spheres of alien thought!" Why, the very notion was bizarre. And yet somehow it had all happened. *Something* had happened.

His movements had automatically taken him under the shower. And now, as he soaped himself and the warm water cascaded down, he wondered if he ought not to talk it over with Holstrom of psychology or a good practicing psychiatrist. The mental contortions he'd gone through in the past few days would provide material for a whole treatise! But feeling as sound as he did this morning, it was impossible for him to entertain any ideas of serious mental derangement. No, what had happened was just one of those queer, inexplicable spasms of irrationality that can seize the sanest people, perhaps because they *are* so sane—a kind of discharge of long-inhibited morbidity. Too bad, though, that he had bothered Tansy with it, even though it was her own little witchcraft complex, now happily conquered, that had touched it off. Poor kid, she had been working hard to cheer him up last night. It ought to have been the other way around. Well, he would make it up to her.

He shaved leisurely and with enjoyment. The razor behaved perfectly.

As he finished dressing, a doubt struck him. Again he searched his mind, closing his eyes like a man listening for an almost inaudible sound.

Nothing. Not the faintest trace of any morbid fears.

He was whistling as he pushed into the kitchen.

There was no sign of breakfast. Beside the sink were some unwashed glasses, empty bottles, and an ice tray filled with tepid water.

"Tansy!" he called. "Tansy!"

He walked through the house, with the vague apprehension that she might have passed out before getting to bed. They'd been drinking like fish. He went out to the garage and made sure that the car was still there. Maybe she'd walked to the grocer's to get something for breakfast. But he began to hurry as he went back into the house.

This time when he looked in the study he noticed the upset ink bottle, and the scrap of paper just beside it on the edge of the drying black pool. The message had come within an inch of being engulfed.

It was a hurried scrawl—twice the pen point had gouged through the paper—and it broke off in the middle of a sentence, but it was undeniably in Tansy's handwriting.

For a moment it isn't watching me. I didn't realize it would be too strong for me. Not two weeks—two days! Don't try to follow me. Only chance is to do exactly what I tell you. Take four four-inch white—

His eyes traced the smear going out from the black pool and ending in the indistinct print of a hand, and involuntarily his imagination created a scene. Tansy had been scribbling desperately, stealing quick glances over her shoulder. Then *it* had awakened to what she was doing and roughly struck the pen out of her hand, and shaken her. He recalled the grip of those huge horny hands, and winced. And then . . . then she had got together her things, very quietly although there was little chance of him awakening, and she had walked out of the house and down the street. And if she met anyone she knew, she had talked to them gayly, and laughed, because *it* was behind her, waiting for any false move, any attempt at escape.

So she had gone.

He wanted to run out into the street and shout her name.

But the pool of ink had dried to glistening black flakes all around the margin. It must have been spilled hours ago.

Where had she gone, in the night?

Anywhere. Wherever the narrow corridor ended for her, no longer two weeks but only two days long.

In a flash of insight he understood why. If he hadn't been drunk last night, he would have guessed.

One of the oldest and best-established types of conjuration in the world. Transference of evils. Like the medicine man who conjures sickness into a stone, or into an enemy, or into himself—because he is better able to combat it—she had taken his curse upon herself. Shared his drink last night, shared his food. Used a thousand devices to bring them together. It was all so obvious! He racked his brain to recover those last words she had said. "Everything you have is mine? All you have is mine?"

She had meant the doom that had been laid on him.

And he had said, "Yes."

Wait a minute! What the devil was he letting himself think? He raised his eyes to the shelves of soberly bound books. Why, here he was giving way to the same sort of rot he'd been weakly toying with the past few days—now when something serious was at stake. No, no, there was nothing supernatural in this—no *it,* no guardian except a figment of his and her neurotic nerves. What *had* happened was that he had *suggested* all this nonsense to her. He had forced upon her the products of his own morbid imagination. Undoubtedly he had babbled nonsense to her while he was drunk. All his childish fancies. And it had worked on her suggestible nature—she already believing in witchcraft—until she had got the idea of transferring his doom to herself, and had convinced herself that the transference had actually occurred. And then gone off, God knows where.

And that was bad enough.

He found himself looking again at the scrawled message. He automatically asked himself, "Now what the devil are 'four-inch whites'?"

There was a light chime from the front door. He extracted a letter from the mailbox, ripped it open. It was addressed with a soft pencil and the graphite had smeared. But he knew the handwriting.

The message was so jerky and uneven that he was some time reading it. It began and ended in the middle of a sentence.

cords—and a length of gut, a bit of platinum or iridium, a piece of lodestone, a phonograph needle that has only played Scriabin's "Ninth Sonata." Then tie—

"Cords." Of course!

That was all. A continuation of the first message, with its bizarre formula. Had she really convinced herself that there was a guardian watching her, and that she could only communicate during the infrequent moments when she imagined its attention was elsewhere? He knew the answer. When you had an obsession you could convince yourself of anything.

He looked at the postmark. He recognized the name of a town several miles east of Hempnell. He could not think of a soul they knew there, or anything else about the town. His first impulse was to get out the car and rush over. But what could he do when he got there?

He looked again. The phone was ringing. It was Evelyn Sawtelle.

"Is that you, Norman? Please ask Tansy to come to the phone. I wish to speak to her."

"I'm sorry, but she isn't in."

Evelyn Sawtelle did not sound suprised at the answer—her second question came too quickly. "Where is she then? I must get in touch with her."

He thought. "She's out in the country," he said, "visiting some friends of ours. Is there something I can tell her?"

"No, I wish to speak to Tansy. What is your friend's number?"

"They don't have a phone!" he said angrily.

"No? Well, it's nothing of importance." She sounded oddly pleased, as if his anger had given her satisfaction. "I'll call again. I must hurry now. Hervey is so busy with his new responsibilities. Good-by."

He replaced the phone. Now, why the devil—Suddenly an explanation occurred to him. Perhaps Tansy had been seen leaving town, and Evelyn Sawtelle had scented the possibility of some sort of scandal and had wanted to check. Perhaps Tansy had been carrying a suitcase.

He looked in Tansy's dressing room. The small suitcase was gone. Drawers were open. It looked as if she had packed in a hurry. But what about money? He examined his billfold. It was empty. Forty-odd dollars missing.

You could go a long way on forty dollars. The jerky illegibility of the message suggested that it had been written on a train or bus.

The next few hours were very miserable ones for Norman. He checked schedules and found that several busses and trains passed through the town from which Tansy's letter had been sent. He drove to the stations and made guarded inquiries, with no success.

He wanted to do all the things you should do when someone disappears, but he held back. What could he say? "My wife, sir, has disappeared. She is suffering from the delusion that—" And what if she should be found and questioned in her present state of mind, examined by a doctor, before he could get to her?

No, this was something for him to handle alone. But if he did not soon get a clue to where she had gone, he would have no choice. He would have to go to the police, inventing some story to cover the facts.

She had written, "Two days." If she believed that she were doomed to die in two days, might not the belief be enough?

Toward evening he drove back to the house, repressing the chimerical hope that she had returned in his absence. The special-delivery man was just getting into his car. Norman pulled up alongside.

"Anything for Saylor?"

"Yes, sir. It's in the box."

The message was longer this time, but just as difficult to read.

At last its attention is somewhere else. If I control my emotions, it isn't so quick to notice my thoughts. But it was hard for me to post the last letter, Norman, you must do what I tell you. The two days end Sunday midnight. Then the Bay. You must follow all directions. Tie the four cords into a granny, a reef, a cat's-paw, and a carrick bend. Tie the gut in a bowline. Then add—

He looked at the postmark. The place was two hundred miles east. Not on the railroad lines, as far as he could recall. That should narrow down the possibilities considerably.

One word from the letter was repeating itself in his mind, like a musical note struck again and again until it becomes unendurable.

Bay. Bay. Bay. Bay.

The memory came of a hot afternoon years ago. It was just before they were married. They were sitting on the edge of a ramshackle little pier. He remembered the salty, fish smell and the splintery, gray old planks.

"Funny," she had said, looking into the green water, "but

I always used to think that I'd end up down there. Not that I'm afraid of it. I've always swum way out. But even when I was a little girl I'd look at the Bay—maybe green, maybe blue, maybe gray, covered with whitecaps, glittering with moonbeams or shrouded by fog—and I'd think, 'Tansy, the Bay is going to get you, but not for years and years.' Funny, isn't it?''

And he had laughed and put his arms around her tight, and the green water had gone on lapping at the piles trousered with seaweed.

He had been visiting with her family, when her father was still alive, at their home near Bayport on the southern shore of New York Bay.

The narrow corridor ended for her in the Bay, tomorrow night, midnight.

She must be headed for the Bay.

He made several calls—first bus lines, then railroad and air. It was impossible to get a reservation on the airlines, but tonight's train would get him into Jersey City an hour ahead of the bus she must be traveling on, àccording to the deductions he made from the place and time of the postmarks.

He knew he had ample time to pack a few things, cash a check on his way to the station.

He spread her three notes on the table—one in pen, the two in pencil. He reread the crazy incomplete formula.

He frowned. Would a scientist neglect the millionth-and-one possibility? Would the commander of a trapped army disdain a stratagem just because it was not in the books? This stuff looked like gibberish. Yesterday it might have meant something to him emotionally. Today it was just nonsense. But tomorrow night it might conceivably represent a fantastic last chance.

But to compromise with magic.

''Norman, you *must* do what I tell you.'' The words stared at him.

After all, he might need the junk to pacify her if he found her in a near-insane state.

He went into the kitchen and got a ball of white twine.

He rummaged in the closet for his squash racket and cut out the two center strings. That ought to do for gut.

The fireplace had not been cleaned since the stuff from Tansy's dressing table had been burned. He poked around the edges until he found a bit of blackened rock that attracted a needle. Lodestone.

He located the recording of Scriabins's "Ninth Sonata" and started the phonograph, putting in a new needle. He glanced at his wrist watch and paced the room restlessly. Gradually the music took hold of him. It was not pleasant music. There was something tantalizing and exasperating about it, with its droning melody and rocking figures in the base and shakes in the treble and elaborate ornamentation that writhed up and down the piano keyboard. It rasped the nerves.

He began to remember things he had heard about it. Hadn't Tansy told him that Scriabin had called his "Ninth Sonata" a "Black Mass" and had developed an antipathy to playing it? Scriabin, who had conceived a color organ and tried to translate mysticism into music and died of a peculiar lip infection. An innocent-faced Russian with a huge curling mustache. Critical phrases Tansy had repeated to him floated through his mind. "The poisonous 'Ninth Sonata'—the most perfidious piece of music ever conceived—" Ridiculous! How could music be anything but an abstract pattern of tones?

And yet while listening to the thing, one could think differently.

Faster and faster it went. The lovely second theme became infected, was distorted into something raucous and discordant—a march of the damned—a dance of the damned—breaking off suddenly when it had reached an unendurable pitch. Then a repetition of the droning first theme, ending on a soft yet grating note low in the keyboard.

He removed the needle, sealed it in an envelope, and packed it along with the rest of his stuff. Only then did he ask himself why, if he were gathering this junk merely to pacify Tansy, he had bothered to play the "Ninth Sonata" with the needle. Certainly an unused needle would have done just as well. He shrugged his shoulders.

On an afterthought, he tore out of the big dictionary a page carrying an illustrated list of knots.

The telephone stopped him as he was going out.

"Oh, Professor Saylor, would you mind calling Tansy to the phone?" Mrs. Carr's voice was very amicable.

He repeated what he had told Mrs. Sawtelle.

"I'm glad she's having a rest in the country," said Mrs. Carr. "You know, Professor Saylor, I don't think that Tansy's been looking so well lately. I've been a little worried. You're sure she's all right?"

At just that moment, without any warning whatever, another voice cut in.

"What's the idea of checking up on me? Do you think I'm a child? I know what I'm doing!"

"Be quiet!" said Mrs. Carr, sharply. Then in her sweet voice, "I think someone must have cut in on us. Good-by, Professor Saylor."

The line went dead. Norman frowned. That second voice had sounded remarkably like Evelyn Sawtelle's.

He picked up his suitcase and walked out.

CHAPTER XIII

THE BUS DRIVER they pointed out to Norman in Jersey City had thick shoulders and sleepy, competent-looking eyes. He was standing by the wall, smoking a cigarette.

"Sure, she must have been with me," he told Norman after thinking a moment. "A pretty woman, on the small side, in a gray dress, with a silver brooch like you mentioned. One suitcase. Light pigskin. I figured her out as going to see someone who was very sick or had been in an accidnet, maybe."

Norman curbed his impatience. If it had not been for the hour-and-a-half delay outside Jersey City, his train would have been here well ahead of the bus, instead of twenty minutes behind it.

He said, "I want, if possible, to get a line on where she went after she left your bus. The men at the desk can't help me."

The driver looked at Norman. But, he did not say, "What-cha wanta know for?"—for which Norman was grateful. He seemed to decide that Norman was okay.

He said, "I can't be sure, mister, but there was a local bus going down the shore. I think she got on that."

"Would it stop at Bayport?"

The driver nodded.

"How long since it left?"

"About twenty minutes."

"Could I get to Bayport ahead of it? If I took a cab?"

"Just about. If you wanted to pay the bill there and back—and maybe a little extra—I think Alec could take you." He waved casually at a man sitting in a cab just beyond the station. "Mind you, mister, I can't say for certain she got on the shore bus."

"That's all right. Thanks a lot."

In the glow of the street lamp Alec's foxy eyes were more openly curious than the bus driver's, but he did not make any comments.

"I can do it," he said cheerfully, "but we haven't any time to waste. Jump in."

The shore highway led through lonely stretches of marsh and wasteland. Occasionally Norman caught the sibilant rustle of the leagues of tall stiff seagrass, and amid the chemical stenches of industy, a brackish tang from the dark inlets crossed by long low bridges. The odor of the Bay.

Indistinctly he made out factories, oil refineries, and scattered houses.

They passed three or four buses without Alec making any comment. He was paying close attention to the road.

After a long while Alec said, "That should be her."

A constellation of red and green taillights was vanishing over the rise ahead.

"About three miles to Bayport," he continued. "What shall I do?"

"Just get to Bayport a little ahead of her, and stop at the bus station."

"Okay."

They overtook the bus and swung around it. The windows were too high for Norman to see any of the occupants. Besides, the interior lights were out.

As they drew ahead, Alec nodded comfirmingly, "That's her, all right."

The bus station at Bayport was also the railway depot. Vaguely Norman remembered the loosely planked platform, the packed cinders between it and the railway tracks. The depot was smaller and dingier than he recalled, though it still boasted the grotesque ornamental carpentry of the days when Bayport had been a summer resort for New York's rich. The windows of the depot were dark but there were several cars and a long local cab drawn up and there were some men standing around talking in low voices and a couple of soldiers, from Fort Monmouth on nearby Sandy Hook, he supposed.

He had time to scent the salt air, with its faint and not unpleasant trace of fishiness. Then the bus pulled in.

Several passengers stepped down, looking around to spot the people waiting for them.

Tansy was the third. She was staring straight ahead. She was carrying the pigskin suitcase.

"Tansy," he said.

She did not look at him. He noted a large black stain on her right hand, and remembered the spilled ink on his study table.

"Tansy!" he said. "Tansy!"

She walked straight past him, so close that her sleeve brushed his.

"Tansy, what's the matter with you?"

He had turned and hurried after her. She was headed for the local cab. He was conscious of a silence and of curious unfriendly glances. They made him angry.

She did not slacken her pace. He grabbed her elbow and pulled her around. He heard a remonstratory murmur behind him.

"Tansy, stop acting this way! Tansy!"

Her face looked frozen. She stared past him without a hint of recognition in her eyes.

That infuriated him. He did not pause to think. Accumulated tensions prodded him into an explosion. He grabbed both elbows and shook her. She still looked past him, completely aloof—a perfect picture of an aristocratic woman enduring brutality. If she had yelled and fought him, the men might not have interfered.

He was jerked back.

"Lay off her!"

"Who do you think you are, anyway?"

She stood there, with maddening composure. He noticed a scrap of paper flutter out of her hand. Then her eyes met his and he seemed to see fear in them; then he felt a slight, queer shock, as if something had passed from her eyes to his; simultaneously with that and with the pricking of his scalp, there seemed to rise up behind her, but for one moment only a shaggy black form twice her height, with hulking shoulders, outstretched massive hands, and dully glowing eyes.

For one moment only, though. When she turned away, she was alone. Though he did fancy that her shadow on the planking was swollen out and shot up to a size that the position of the street lamp would not account for. Then they swung him around and he could no longer see her.

In a queer sort of daze—for the kind of hallucination he had just experienced mixes badly with any other emotion—he listened to them jabber at him.

"I ought to take a crack at you," he finally heard someone say.

"All right," he replied in a flat voice. "They're holding my hands."

He heard Alec's voice. "Say, what's going on here?" Alec sounded cautious, but not unfriendly, as if he were thinking. "The guy's my fare, but I don't know anything about him."

One of the soldiers spoke. "Where's the lady? She doesn't seem to be making any complaint."

"Yeah, where is she?"

"She got in Jake's cab and drove off," someone volunteered.

"Maybe he had a good reason for what he did," said the soldier.

Norman felt the attitude of the crowd change.

One of the men holding him retorted, ''Nobody's got a right to treat a lady that way.'' But the other slackened his grip and asked Norman, ''How about it? Did you have a reason for doing that?''

''I did. But it's my business.''

He heard a woman's voice, high-pitched, ''A lot of fuss over nothing!'' and a man's, richly sardonic. ''Mix in family quarrels—!''

Grumbling, the two men let him go.

''But mind you,'' said the more belligerent one, ''if she'd stuck around and complained, I'd sure have taken a crack at you.''

''All right,'' said Norman, ''in that case you would have.'' His eyes were searching for the scrap of paper.

''Can anyone tell me the address she gave the cab driver?'' he asked at random.

One or two shook their heads. The others ignored the question. Their feelings toward him had not changed enough to make them cooperative. And very likely, in the excitement, no one had heard.

Silently the little crowd drifted apart. People waited until they got out of earshot before beginning to argue about what had happened. Most of the cars drove off. The two soldiers wandered over to the benches in front of the depot, so they could sit down while they waited for their bus or train. Norman was alone except for Alec.

He located the scrap of paper in one of the slots between the worn planks. It had almost slipped through.

He took it over to the cab and studied it.

He heard Alec say, ''Well, where do we go now?'' Alec sounded dubious.

He glanced at his watch. Ten thirty-five. Not quite an hour and a half until midnight. There were a lot of things he could do to try and find Tansy, but he could not do more than a couple of them in that time. He thoughts moved sluggishly, almost painfully, as if that awful thing he had seemed to see behind Tansy had hurt his brain.

He looked around at the dim buildings. The seaward halves of some of the street lamps still showed traces of black paint from the old wartime dimout. Up a side street there were signs of life. He looked at the scrap of paper.

He thought of Tansy. He thought hard. It was a question oi what might help her most, of what his deepest loyalty to her must now direct him to do. Of course he could go chasing up and down along the shore, along the railroad tracks, though Lord knew to what point the taxi had taken her. He might be able to locate the old pier where they'd gone swimming and try waiting there. Or he could wait for the taxi she'd taken to come back. And he might go to the police, convince them if he could that his wife intended suicide, get them to help him search.

But he also thought of other things. He thought of her confession of witchcraft, of how he had burned the last "hand," of the sudden telephone calls from Theodore Jennings and Margaret Van Nice, of the flurry of ill-will and undesired revelations that had struck him at the college. He thought of Jennings' asinine attempt on his life, of the recordings of a bull-roarer, the photograph of a dragon, and the stick-figure of tarot cards. He thought of the death of Totem, of the seven-branched lightning bolt, of his sudden attack of accident-proneness and suicidal fancies. He thought of the hallucination he had had, while drunk, of something gripping his shoulder and shutting off his speech. He thought of the hallucination he had had just now of something behind Tansy. He thought hard.

He looked again at the scrap of paper.

He came to a decision.

"I think there's a hotel on the main street," he told Alec. "You can drive me there."

CHAPTER XIV

"Eagle hotel," read the black-edged gold letters on the plateglass window, behind which the narrow lobby with its half-dozen empty chairs was nakedly revealed.

He told Alec to wait, and took a room for the night. The clerk was an old man in a shiny blue coat. Norman saw from the register that no one else had checked in recently. He carried his bag up to the room and immediately returned to the lobby.

"I haven't been here for ten years," he told the clerk. "I believe there is a cemetery about five blocks down the street, away from the Bay?"

The old man's sleepy eyes blinked wide open.

"Bayport Cemetery? Just three blocks, and then a block and a half to the left. But—" He made a vague questioning noise in his throat.

"Thank you," said Norman.

After a moment's thought, he paid off Alec, who took the money and with obvious relief kicked his cab into life. Norman walked down the main street, away from the Bay.

After the first block there were no more stores. In this direction, Bayport petered out quickly. Most of the houses were dark. And after he turned left there were no more streets lights.

The gates of the cemetery were locked. He felt his way along the wall, behind the masking shrubbery, trying to make as little noise as possible, until he found a scrubby tree whose lowest branch could bear his weight. He got his hands on the top of the wall, scrambled up, and cautiously let himself down on the other side.

Behind the wall it was very dark. There was a sound, as if he had disturbed some small animal. More by feeling than sight he located a headstone. It was a thin one, worn, mossy toward the base, and tilted at an angle. Probably from the middle of last century. He dug into the earth with his hand, and filled an envelope he took from his pocket.

He got back over the wall, making what seemed a great deal of noise in the shrubbery. But the street was empty as before.

On his way back to the hotel he looked up at the sky, located the Pole Star, and calculated the orientation of his room.

As he crossed the lobby, he felt the curious gaze of the old clerk boring into him.

His room was in darkness. Chill salt air was pouring through the open window. He locked the door, shut the window, pulled down the blind, and switched on the light—a glaring overhead which revealed the room in all its dingy severity. A cradle phone struck the sole modern note.

He took the envelope out of his pocket and weighted it in his hand. His lips curled in a peculiarly bitter smile. Then he re-read the scrap of paper that had fluttered from Tansy's hand.

a small quantity of graveyard dirt and wrap all in a piece of flannel, wrapping widdershins. Tell it to stop me. Tell it to bring me to you.

Graveyard dirt. That was what he had found in Tansy's

dressing table. It had been the beginning of all this. Now he was fetching it himself.

He looked at his watch. Eleven twenty.

He cleared the small table and set it in the center of the room, jabbing in his penknife to mark the edge facing east. "Widdershins," meant "against the sun"—from west to east.

He placed the necessary ingredients on the table, cutting a short strip of flannel from the hem of his bathrobe, and fitted together the four sections of Tansy's note. The distasteful, bitter smile did not leave his lips.

Taken together, the significant portions of the note read?

Take four lengths of four-inch white cord and a length a gut, a bit of platinum or iridium, a piece of lodestone, a phonograph needle that has only played Scriabins's "Ninth Sonata." Tie the four white cords into a granny, a reef, a cat's-paw, and a carrick bend. Tie the gut in a bowline. Add a small quantity of graveyard dirt, and wrap it all in a piece of flannel, wrapping widdershins. Tell it to stop me. Tell it to bring me to you.

In general outline, it was similar to a hundred recipes for Negro tricken-bags he had seen or been told about. The phonograph needle, the knots, and one or two other items were obvious "white" additions.

And it was all on the same level as the mental operations of a child or neurotic adult who religiously steps on, or avoids, sidewalk cracks.

A clock outside bonged the half-hour.

Norman sat there looking at the stuff. It was hard for him to begin. It would have been different, he told himself, if he were doing it for a joke or a thrill, or if he were one of those people who dope up their minds with morbid supernaturalism—who like to play around with magic because it's medieval and because illuminated manuscripts look pretty. But to tackle it in dead seriousness, to open your mind deliberately to superstition—that was to join hands with the forces pushing the world back into the dark ages, to cancel the term "science" out of the equation.

But, behind Tansy, he had seen that thing. Of course it had been an hallucination. But when hallucinations start behaving like realities, with a score of coincidences to back them up, even a scientist has to face the possibility that he may have to treat them like realities. And when hallucinations begin to threaten you and yours in a direct physical way—

No, more than that. When you must keep faith with someone you love. He reached out for the first length of cord and tied the ends together in a granny.

When he came to the cat's-paw, he had to consult the page he had torn from the dictionary. After a couple of false starts he managed it.

But on the carrick bend he was all thumbs. It was a simple knot but no matter how he went about it, he could not get it to look like the illustration. Sweat broke out on his forehead. "Very close in the room," he told himself. "I'm still over-heated from rushing about." The skin on his fingertips felt an inch thick. The ends of the cord kept eluding them. He remembered how Tansy's fingers had rippled through the knots.

Eleven forty-one. The phonograph needle started to roll off the table. He dropped the cord and laid the phonograph needle against his fountain pen, so it would not roll. Then he started again on the knot.

For a moment he thought he must have picked up the gut, the cord seemed so stiff and unresponsive. Incredible what nervousness can do to you, he told himself. His mouth was dry. He swallowed with difficulty.

Finally, by keeping his eyes on the illustration and imitating it step for step, he managed to tie a carrick bend. All the while he felt as if there were more between his fingers than a cord, as if he were manipulating against a great inertia. Just as he finished, he felt a slight prickly chill, like the onset of fever, and the light overhead seemed to dim a trifle. Eye-strain.

The phonograph needle was rolling in the opposite direction, spinning faster and faster. He slapped his hand down on it, missed it, slapped again, caught it at the edge of the table.

Just like a Ouija board, he told himself. You try to keep your fingers, poised on the planchette, perfectly motionless. As a result, muscular tensions accumulate. They reach the breaking point. Seemingly without any volition on your part, the planchette begins to roll and skid about on its three little legs, traveling from letter to letter. Same thing here. Nervous and muscular tensions made it difficult for him to tie knots. Obeying a universal tendency, he projected the difficulty into the cord. And, by elbow and knee pressure, he had been doing some unconscious table tipping.

Between his fingers, the phonograph needle seemed to vibrate, as if it were a tiny part of a great machine. There was a very faint suggestion of electric shock. Unbidden, the torturesome, clangorous chords of the "Ninth Sonata" began to sound in his mind. Rot! One well-known symptom of extreme nervousness ia a tingling in the fingers, often painfully intense. But his throat was dry and his snort of bitter contempt sounded choked.

He pinned the needle in the flannel for greater safety.

Eleven forty-seven. Reaching for the gut, his fingers felt shaky and weak as if he just climbed a hundred-foot rope hand over hand. The stuff looked normal, but it was slimy to the touch, as if it had just been dragged from the beast's belly and twisted into shape. And for some moments he had been conscious of an acrid, almost metallic odor replacing the salt smell of the Bay. Tactual and olfactory hallucinations joining in with the visual and auditory, he told himself. He could still hear the "Ninth Sonata."

He knew how to tie a bowline backwards, and it should have been easier since the gut was not as stiff as it ought to be, but he felt there were other forces manipulating it or other mentalites trying to give orders to his fingers, so that the gut was trying to tie itself into a slip-knot, a reef, a half hitch—anything but a bowline. His fingers ached, his eyes were heavy with an abnormal fatigue. He was working against a mounting inertia, a crushing inertia. He remembered Tansy telling him that night when she had confessed her witchcraft to him: "There's a law of reaction in all conjuring—like the kick of a gun—" Eleven fifty-two.

With a great effort, he canalized his mental energy, focused his attention only on the knot. His numb fingers began to move in an odd rhythm, a rhythm of the "Ninth Sonata," *piu vivo*. The bowline was tied.

The overhead light dimmed markedly, throwing the whole room into sooty gloom. Hysterical blindness, he told himself—and small town power systems are always going on the blink. It was very cold now, so cold that he fancied he could see his breath. And silent, terribly silent. Against that silence he could feel and hear the rapid drumming of his heart, acclerating unendurably to the thundering, swirling rhythm of the misic.

Then, in one instant of diabolic, paralyzing insight, he knew that *this* was sorcery. No mere puttering about with ridiculous medieval implements, no effortless sleight of hand, but a straining, back-breaking struggle to keep control of *forces summoned*, of which the objects he manipulated were only the symbols. Outside the walls of the room, outside the walls of his skull, outside the impalpable energy-walls of his mind, he felt those forces gathering, swelling up, dreadfully expectant, waiting for him to make a false move so that they could crush him.

He could not believe it. He did not believe it. Yet somehow he *had* to believe it.

The only question was—would he be able to stay in control?

Eleven fifty-seven. He started to gather the objects together on the flannel. The needle jumped to the lodestone, dragging the flannel with it, and clung. It shouldn't have; it had been a foot away. He took a pinch of graveyard dirt. Between finger and thumb, each separate particle seemed to crawl, like a tiny maggot. He sensed that something was missing. He could not remember what it was. He fumbled for the formula. A current of air was blowing the scraps of paper off the table. He sensed an eager, inward surge of the forces outside, as if they knew he was failing. He clutched at the papers, managed to pin them down. Bending close, he made out the words "platinum or iridium." He jabbed his fountain pen against the table, broke off the nib, and added it to the other objects.

He stood at the side of the table away from the knife that marked the east, trying to steady his shaking hands against the edge. His teeth were chattering. The room was utterly dark now except for the impossible bluish light that beat through the window shade. Surely the street light wasn't that mercury-vapor hue.

Abruptly the strip of flannel started to curl like a strip of heated gelatine, to roll itself up from east to west, *with* the sun.

He jerked forward, got his hand inside the flannel before it closed, drew it apart—in his numb hands it seemed like metal—and rolled it up against the sun, widdershins.

The silence was intensified. Even the sound of his beating heart was cut off. He knew that something was listening with a terrible intentness for his command, and that something was hoping with an even more terrible avidity that he would not be able to utter that command.

Somewhere a clock was booming—or was it not a clock, but the secret sound of time? Nine—ten—eleven—twelve.

His tongue stuck to the roof of his mouth. He kept on choking soundlessly. It seemed to him that the walls of the room were closer to him than they had been a minute before.

Then, in a dry, croaking voice he managed: "Stop Tansy. Bring her here."

Norman felt the room shake, the floor buckle, and lift under his feet, as if an earthquake had visited New Jersey. Darkness became absolute. The table, or some force erupting from the table, seemed to rise and strike him. He felt himself flung back onto something soft.

Then the forces were gone. In all things, tension gave way

to limpness. Sound and light returned. He was sprawled across the bed. On the table was a little flannel packet, no longer of any consequence.

He felt as if he had been doped, or were waking after a debauch. There was no inclination to do anything. Emotion was absent.

Outwardly everything was the same. Even his mind, with automatic rationality, could wearily take up the thankless task of explaining his experiences on a scientific basis— weaving an elaborate web in which psychosis, hallucination, and improbably coincidences were the strands.

But inwardly something had changed, and would never change back.

Considerable time passed.

He heard stept mounting the stairs, then in the hall. They made a *squish-squish* sound, as if the shoes were soaking wet.

They stopped outside his door.

He crossed the room, turned the key in the lock, opened the door.

A strand of seaweed was caught in the silver brooch. The gray suit was dark now and heavy with water, except for one spot which had started to dry and was faintly dusted with salt. The odor of the Bay was intimate and close. There was another strand of seaweed clinging to one ankle against the wrinkled stockings.

Around the stained shoes, a little pool of water was forming.

His eyes traced the wet footprints down the hall. At the head of the stairs the old clerk was standing, one foot still on the last step. He was carrying a small pigskin suitcase, waterstained.

"What's this all about?" he quavered, when he saw that Norman was looking at him. "You didn't tell me you were expecting your wife. She looks like she'd thrown herself in the Bay. We don't want anything queer happening in this hotel—anything wrong."

"It's quite all right," said Norman, prolonging the moment before he would have to look in her face. "I'm sorry I forgot to tell you. May I have the bag?"

"—only last year we had a suicide,"—the old clerk did not seem to realize he was speaking his thoughts aloud— "bad for the hotel." His voice trailed off. He looked at Norman, gathered himself together, and came hesitatingly down the hall. When he was a few steps away, he stopped, reached out and put down the suitcase, turned, and walked rapidly away.

Unwillingly, Norman raised his eyes until they were on a level with hers.

The face was pale, very pale, and without expression. The lips were tinged with blue. Wet hair was plastered against the cheeks. A thick lock crossed one eye socket, like a curtain, and curled down toward the throat. One eye stared at him, without recognition. And no hand moved to brush the lock of hair away from the other.

From the hem of the skirt, water was dripping.

The lips parted. The voice had the monotonous murmur of water.

"You were too late," the voice said. "You were a minute too late."

CHAPTER XV

FOR A THIRD TIME they had come back to the same question. Norman had the maddening sensation of following a robot that was walking in a huge endless circle and always treading on precisely the same blades of grass as it retraced its path.

With the hopeless conviction that he would not get any further this time, he asked the question again: "But how can you lack consciousness, and at the same time *know* that you lack consciousness? If your mind is blank, you cannot at the same time be aware that your mind is blank."

The hands of his watch were creeping toward three in the morning. The chill and sickliness of night's lowest ebb pervaded the dingy hotel room. Tansy sat stiffly, wearing Norman's bathrobe and fleece-lined slippers, with a blanket over her knees and a bath towel wrapped around her head. They should have made her look childlike and perhaps even artlessly attractive. They did not. If you were to unwind the towel you would find the top of the skull sawed off and the brains removed, an empty bowl—that was the illusion Norman experienced every time he made the mistake of looking into her eyes.

The pale lips parted. ''I know nothing. I only speak. They have taken away my soul. But my voice is a function of my body.''

You could not say the voice was patiently explanatory. It was too empty and colorless even for that. The words, clearly enunciated and evenly spaced, all sounded alike. They were like the noise of a machine.

The last thing he wanted to do was hammer questions at this stiff pitiful figure, but he felt that at all costs he must awaken some spark of feeling in the masklike face; he must find some intelligible starting point before his own mind could begin to work effectually.

''But Tansy, if you can talk about the present situation, you must be aware of it. You're here in this room with me!''

The toweled head shook once, like that of a mechanical doll.

''Nothing is here with you but a body. 'I' is not here.''

His mind automatically corrected ''is'' to ''am'' before he realized that there had been no grammatical error. He trembled.

''You mean,'' he asked, ''that you can see or hear nothing? That there is just a blackness?''

Again that simple mechanical headshake, which carried more absolute conviction than the most heated protestations.

''My body sees and hears perfectly. It has suffered no injury. It can function in all particulars. But there is nothing inside. There is not even a blackness.''

His tired, fumbling mind jumped to the subject of behavioristic psychology and its fundamental assertion that human reactions can be explained completely and satisfactorily without once referring to consciousness—that it need not even be assumed that consciousness exists. Here was the perfect proof. And yet not so perfect, for the behavior of this body lacked every one of those little mannerisms whose sum is personality. The way Tansy used to squint when thinking through a difficult question. The familiar quirk at the corners of her mouth when she felt flattered or slyly amused. All gone. Even the quick triple headshake he knew so well, with the slight rabbity wrinkling of the nose, had become a robot's "No."

Her sensory organs still responded to stimuli. They sent impulses to the brain, where they traveled about and gave rise to impulses which activated glands and muscles, including the motor organs of speech. But that was all. None of those intangible flurries we call consciousness hovered around the webwork of nervous activity in the cortex. What had imparted style—Tansy's style, like no one else's—to every movement and utterance of the body, was gone. There was left only a physiological organism, without sign or indication of personality. Not even a mad or an idiot soul—yes! why not use that old term now that it had an obvious specific meaning?—peered from the gray-green eyes which winked at intervals with machine-like regularity, but only to lubricate the cornea, nothing more.

He felt a grim sort of relief go through him, now that he had been able to picture Tansy's condition in definite terms. But the picture itself—his mind veered to the memory of a newspaper story about an old man who had kept locked in his bedroom for years the body of a young woman whom he loved and who had died of an incurable disease. He had maintained the body in an astonishing state of preservation by wax and other means, they said, had talked to it every night and morning, had been convinced that he would some day reanimate it complete—until they found out and took it away from him and buried it.

He suddenly grimaced. Damn it all, he commented inwardly, why did he let his mind go off on these wild fancies, when it was obvious that Tansy was suffering from an unusual nervous condition, a strange self-delusion?

Obvious.

Wild fancies?

"Tansy," he asked, "when your soul went, why didn't you die?"

"Usually the soul lingers to the end, unable to escape, and vanishes or dies when the body dies," the voice answered, its words as evenly spaces as if timed to a metronome. "But He

Who Walks Behind was tearing at mine. There was the weight of green water against my face. I knew it was midnight. I knew you had failed. In that moment of despair, He Who Walks Behind was able to draw forth my soul. In the same moment Your Agent's arms were about me, lifting me toward the air. My soul was close enough to know what had happened, yet not close enough to return. Its doubled anguish was the last memory it imprinted on my brain. Your Agent and He Who Walks Behind concluded that each had obtained the thing he had been sent for, so there was no struggle between them."

The picture created in Norman's mind was so shockingly vivid that it seemed incredible that it could have been produced by the words of a mere physiological machine. And yet only a physiological machine could have told the story with such total restraint.

"Is there nothing that touches you?" he asked abruptly in a loud voice, gripped by an intolerable spasm of anguish at the emptiness of her eyes. "Haven't you a single emotion left?"

"Yes. One." This time it was not a robot's headshake, but a robot's nod. For the first time there was a stir of feeling, a hint of motivation. The tip of a pallid tongue licked hungrily around the pale lips. "I want my soul."

He caught his breath. Now that he had succeeded in awakening a feeling in her, he hated it. There was something so animal about it, so like some light-sensitive worm greedily wriggling toward the sunlight.

"I want my soul," the voice repeated mechanically, tearing at his emotions more than any plaintive or whining accents could have done. "At the last moment, although it could not return, my soul implanted that one emotion in me. It knew what awaited it. It knew there are things that can be done to a soul. It was very much afraid."

He ground out the words between his teeth. "Where do you think your soul is?"

"She has it. The woman with the small dull eyes."

He looked at her. Something began to pound inside him.

He knew it was rage, and for the moment he didn't care whether it was sane rage or not.

"Evelyn Sawtelle?" he asked huskily.

"Yes. But it is not wise to speak of her by name."

His hand shot out for the phone. He had to do something definite, or lose control of himself completely.

After a time he roused the night clerk and got the local operator.

"Yes, sir," came the singsong voice. "Hempnell 1284. You wish to make a person-to-person call to Evelyn Sawtelle—E-V-E-L-Y-N S-A-W-T-E-L-L-E, sir? . . . Will you please hang up and wait? It will take considerable time to make a connection."

"I want my soul. I want to go to that woman. I want to go to Hempnell." Now that he had touched off the blind hunger in the creature facing him, it persisted. He was reminded of a phonograph needle caught in the same groove, or a mechanical toy turned on to a new track by a little push.

"We'll go there all right." It was still hard for him to control his breathing. "We'll get it back."

"But I must start for Hempnell soon. My clothes are ruined by the water. I must have the maid clean and press them."

With a slow, even movement she got to her feet and started toward the phone.

"But, Tansy," he objected involuntarily, "it's three in the morning. You can't get a maid now."

"But my clothes must be cleaned and pressed. I must start for Hempnell soon."

The words might have been those of an obstinate woman, sulky and selfish. But they had less tone than a sleepwalker's.

She kept on toward the phone. Although he did not anticipate that he would do it, he shrank out of her way, pressing close against the side of the bed.

"But even if there is a maid," he said, "she won't come at this hour."

The pallid face turned toward him incuriously.

"The maid will be a woman. She will come when she hears me."

Then she was talking to the night clerk. "Is there a maid in the hotel? . . . Send her to my room. . . . Then ring her. . . . I cannot wait until morning. . . . I need her at once. . . . I cannot tell you the reason. . . . Thank you."

There was a long wait while he heard faintly the repeated ringing at the other end of the line. He could imagine the sleepy, surly voice that finally answered.

"Is this the maid? . . . Come at once to Room 37." He could almost catch the indignant answer. Then— "Can't you hear my voice? Don't you realize my condition? . . . Yes. . . . Come at once." And she replaced the phone in its cradle.

"Tansy—" he began. His eyes were on her still and once again he found himself making a halting preamble, although he had not intended to. "You are able to hear and answer my questions?"

"I can answer questions. I have been answering questions for three hours."

But—logic prompted wearily—if she can remember what has been happening these last three hours, then surely—And yet, what is memory but a track worn in the nervous system? In order to explain memory you don't need to bring in consciousness.

Quit banging your head against that stone wall, you fool!—came another inward prompting. You've look in her eyes, haven't you? Well, then, get on with it!

"Tansy," he asked, "when you say that Evelyn Sawtelle has your soul, what do you mean?"

"Just that."

"Don't you mean that she, and Mrs. Carr and Mrs. Gunnison too, have some sort of psychological power over you, that they hold you in a kind of emotional bondage?"

"No."

"But your soul—"

"—is my soul."

"Tansy." He hated to bring up this subject, but he felt he must. "Do you believe that Evelyn Sawtelle is a witch, that she is going through the motions of practicing witchcraft, just as you did?"

"Yes."

"And Mrs. Carr and Mrs. Gunnison?"

"They too."

"You mean you believe they're doing the same things that you did—laying spells and making charms, making use of their husbands' special knowledge, trying to protect their husbands and advance their careers?"

"They go further."

"What do you mean?"

"They use black magic as well as white. They don't care if they hurt or torment or kill."

"Why are they different in that way?"

"Witches are like people. There are the sanctimonious, self-worshipping, self-deceiving ones, the ones who believe their ends justify any means."

"Do you believe that all three of them are working together against you?"

"Yes."

"Why?"

"Because they hate me."

"Why?"

"Partly they hate me because of you and what your advancement might do to their husbands and themselves. But more than that, they hate me because they sense that my inmost standards are different from theirs. They sense that, though I conform on the surface, I do not really worship respectability. Witches, you see, are apt to have the same gods as people. They fear me because I do not bow down to Hempnell. Though Mrs. Carr, I think, has an additional reason."

"Tansy," he began and hesitated. "Tansy, how do you think it happens that these three women are witches?"

"It happens."

There was a silence in the room then, as Norman's thoughts dully revolved around the topic of paranoia. Then, "But Tansy," he said with an effort, "don't you see what that implies? The idea that all women are witches."

"Yes."

"But how can you ever—"

"Ssh." There was no more expression to the sound than an escape of steam from a radiator, but it shut up Norman. "She is coming."

"Who?"

"The maid. Hide, and I will show you something."

"Hide?"

"Yes." She came toward him and he involuntarily backed away from her. His hand touched a door. "The closet?" he asked, wetting his lips.

"Yes. Hide there, and I will prove something to you."

Norman heard footsteps in the hall. He hesitated a moment, frowning, then did as she asked him.

"I'll leave the door a little ajar," he said. "See, like this."

The robot nod was his only answer.

There was a tapping at the door. Tansy's footsteps, the sound of the door opening.

"Y'ast for me, ma'am?" Contrary to his expectations, the voice was young. It sounded as if she had swallowed as she spoke.

"Yes. I want you to clean and press some things of mine. They've been in salt water. They're hanging on the edge of the bathtub. Go and get them."

The maid came into his line of vision. She would be fat in a few years, he thought, but she was handsome now, though puffed with sleep. She had pulled on a dress, but her feet were in slippers and her hair was snarly.

"Be careful with the suit. It's wool," came Tansy's voice, sounding just as toneless as when it had been directed at him. "And I want them within an hour."

Norman half expected to hear an objection to this unreasonable request, but there was none. The girl said, "All rightie, ma'am.'' and walked rapidly out of the bathroom, the damp clothes hurriedly slung over one arm, as if her one object were to get away before she was spoken to again.

"Wait a minute, girl. I want to ask you a question.'' The voice was somewhat louder this time. That was the only change, but it had a startling effect of command.

The girl hesitated, then swung around unwillingly, and Norman got a good look at her face. He could not see Tansy—the closet door just cut her off—but he could see the fear come to the surface of the girl's sleep-creased face.

"Yes, ma'am?'' she managed.

There was a considerable pause. He could tell from the way the girl shrank, hugging the damp clothes tight to her body, that Tansy had lifted her eyes and was looking at her.

Finally: "You know The Easy Way to Do Things? The Ways to Get and Guard?''

Norman could have sworn that the girl gave a start at the second phrase. But she only shook her head quickly, and mumbled, "No, ma'am. I . . . I don't know what you're talking about.''

"You mean you never learned How to Make Wishes Work? You don't conjure, or spell or hex? You don't know the Art?''

The time the "No'' was almost inaudible. The girl was trying to look away and failing.

"I think you are lying.''

The girl twisted, hands tightly clutching her overlapping arms. She looked so frightened that Norman wanted to go out and stop it, but curiosity held him rigid.

The girl's resistance broke. "Please, ma'am, we're not supposed to tell.''

"You may tell me. What Procedures do you use?''

The girl's perplexity at the new word looked real.

"I don't know anything about that, ma'am. I don't do much. Like when my boyfriend was in the army, I did things to keep him from getting shot or hurt, and I've spelled him so that he'll keep away from other women. And I kin annernt

with erl for sickness. Honest, I don't do much, ma'am. And
it don't always work. And lots of things I can't get that way.''
Her words had begun to run away with her.

"Very well. Where did you learn to do this?"

"Some I learned from Ma when I was a kid. And some
from Mrs. Neidel—she got spells against bullets from her
grandmother who had a family in some European war way
back. But most women won't tell you anything. And some
spells I kind of figure out myself, and try different ways until
they work. You won't tell on me, ma'am?"

"No. Look at me now. What has happened to me?"

"Honest, ma'am, I don't know. Please, don't make me
say it.'' The girl's terror and reluctance were so obviously
genuine that Norman felt a surge of anger at Tansy. Then he
remembered that the thing beyond the door was incapable of
either cruelty or kindness.

"I want you to tell me."

"I don't know how to say it, ma'am. But you're . . .
you're *dead*.'' Suddenly she threw herself at Tansy's feet.
"Oh, please, please, don't take my soul! Please!"

"I would not take your soul. You would get much the best
of that bargain. You may go away now.''

"Oh, thank you, thank you.'' The girl hastily gathered up
the scattered clothes. "I'll have them all ready for you very
soon. Really I will." And she hurried out.

Only when he moved, did Norman realize that his muscles
were stiff and aching from those few taut minutes of peering.
The robed and toweled figure was sitting in exactly the same
position as when he had last seen it, hands loosely folded,
eyes still directed toward where the girl had been standing.

"If you knew all this,'' he asked simply, his mind in a kind
of trance from what he had witnessed, "why were you
willing to stop last week when I asked you?"

"There are two sides to every woman.'' It might have
been a mummy dispensing elder wisdom. "One is rational,
like a man. The other knows. Men are artificially isolated
creatures like islands in a sea of magic, protected by their

rationality and by the devices of their women. Their isolation gives them greater forcefulness in thought and action, but the women know. Women might be able to rule the world openly, but they do not want the work or the responsibility. And men might learn to excel them in the Art. Even now there may still be male sorcerers, but very few.

"Last week I suspected much that I did not tell you. But the rational side is strong in me, and I wanted to be close to you in all ways. Like many women, I was not certain. And when I destroyed my charms and guards, I became temporarily blind to sorcery. Like a person used to large doses of a drug, I was uninfluenced by small doses. Rationality was dominant. I enjoyed a few days of false security. Then rationality itself proved to me that you were the victim of sorcery. And during my journey here I learned much, partly from what He Who Walks Behind let slip." She paused and added, with the blank innocent cunning of a child, "Shall we go back to Hempnell now?"

The phone rang. It was the night clerk, almost incoherent in his agitation, babbling threateningly about the police and eviction. To pacify him, Norman had to promise to come down at once.

The old man was waiting at the foot of the stairs.

"Look here, mister," he began, shaking a finger, "I want to know what's going on. Just now Sissy came down from your room white as a sheet. She wouldn't tell me anything, but she was trembling like all get-out. Sissy's my granddaughter. I got her this job, and I'm responsible for her.

"I know what hotels are. I've worked in 'em all my life. And I know the kind of people that come to them— sometimes men and women working together—and I know the kind of things they try to do to young girls.

"Now I'm not saying anything against you, mister. But it was mighty queer the way your wife came here. I thought when she asked me to call Sissy that she was sick or something. But if she's sick, why haven't you called a doctor? And what are you doing still up at four? Mrs. Thompson in

the next room called to say there was talking in your room—
not loud, but it scared her. I got a right to know what's going
on.''

Norman put on his best classroom manner and blandly
dissected the old man's apprehensions until they began to
look very unsubstantial. Dignity told. With a last show of
grumbling the old man let himself be convinced. As Norman
started upstairs, he was shuffling back to the switchboard.

On the second flight, Norman heard a phone ringing. As
he was walking down the hall, it stopped.

He opened the door. Tansy was standing by the bed,
speaking into the phone, Its dull blackness, curving from
mouth to ear, emphasized the pallor of lips and cheeks and
the whiteness of the toweling.

''This is Tansy Saylor,'' she was saying tonelessly.''I
want my soul.'' A pause. ''Can't you hear me, Evelyn? This
is Tansy Saylor. I want my soul.''

He had completely forgotten the call he had made in a
moment of crazy anger. He no longer had any clear idea of
what he had been going to say.

A low wailing was coming from the phone. Tansy was
talking against it.

''This is Tansy Saylor. I want my soul.''

He stepped forward. The wailing sound had swiftly risen
to a squeal, but mised with it was an intermittent windy
whirring.

He reached out to take the phone. But at that instant Tansy
jerked around and something seemed to happen to the phone.

When a lifeless object begins to act as if it has life, there is
always the possibility of illusion. For instance, there is a trick
of manipulating a pencil that makes it look as if it were being
bent back and forth like a stick of rubber. And Tansy did have
her hand to the phone and was twisting about so rapidly that it
was hard to be sure of anything.

Nevertheless, to Norman it seemed that the phone suddenly became pliable and twisted about like a stumpy black
worm, fastened itself tight to the skin, and dug into Tansy's

chin and into her neck just below the ear, like a double-ended black paw. And with the squeal he seemed to hear a muffled sucking.

His reaction was immediate, involuntary, and startling. He dropped to his knees and ripped the phone cord from the wall. Violet sparks spat from the torn wire. The loose end whipped back with his jerk, seeming to writhe like a wounded snake, and wrapped itself around his forearm. To Norman it seemed that it tightened spasmodically, then re-laxed. He tore it away with a panicky loathing, then stood up.

The phone had fallen to the floor. There seemed to be nothing out of the ordinary about it now. He gave it a little kick. There was a dull *plunk* and it slid solidly across the floor a few inches. He stooped and after hesitating a few moments gingerly touched it. It felt as hard and rigid as it should.

He looked at Tansy. She was standing in the same place. Not an atom of fear showed in her expression. With the unconcernedness of a machine, she had lifted a hand and was slowly massaging her cheek and neck. From the corner of her mouth a few drops of blood were trickling.

Of course, she could have bashed the phone against her teeth and cut her lip that way.

But he had seen—

Still, she might have shaken the phone rapidly, so that it only seemed to become pliable and bend.

But it hadn't looked that way. What he had seen . . . had been impossible.

But so many ''impossible'' things had been happening.

And it *had* been Evelyn Sawtelle at the other end of the phone. He *had* heard the sound of the bull-roarer coming over the phone. Nothing supernatural about that. If the re-cording of a bull-roarer had been played very loudly over the phone it would have sounded just like that. He *couldn't* have been mistaken about it. That was a fact and he must stick to it.

It gave him the emotional cue he needed. Anger. He was almost startled by the surge of hatred that went through him at the thought of that woman with the small dull eyes. For a moment he felt like an inquisitor confronted with evidence of malicious witchcraft. Visions of the rack and the wheel and the boot flitted through his mind. Then that phantasmagoria of the Middle Ages faded, but the anger remained, settling down to a steady pulse of detestation.

Whatever had happened to Tansy, he *knew* that Evelyn Sawtelle and Hulda Gunnison and Flora Carr were responsible. He had too much evidence in their own actions. That was another fact that he must stick to. Whether they were working on Tansy's mind by an incredibly subtle and diabolic campaign of suggestion, or by some unnamed means, they were responsible.

There was no way of getting at them by psychiatry or law. What had happened in the past few days was something that only he, of all the men in the world, could believe or understand. He must fight them himself, using their own weapons against them—that other unnamed means.

In every way he must act as if he believed in that other unnamed means.

Tansy stopped massaging her face. Her tongue licked the lip where the blood was drying.

"Shall we go back to Hempnell now?"

"Yes!"

CHAPTER XVI

THE RHYTHMIC RATTLE and clank of the train was a Machine Age lullaby. Norman could hear the engine snoring. The wide, heat-baked, green fields swinging past the window of the compartment drowsed in the noonday sun. The farms and cattle and horses dotting them here and there were entranced by the heat. He would have liked to doze too, but he knew he would not be able to. And as for—she apparently never slept.

"I want to run over some things," he said. "Interrupt me if you hear anything that sounds wrong or you don't understand."

From the corner of his eye he noted the figure sitting between him and the window nod once.

It occurred to him that there was something terrible about an adaptability that could familiarize him even to—her, so that now, after only a day and a half, he was using her as a kind of thinking machine, asking for her memories and reactions in the same way that a man might direct a servant to put a certain record on the phonograph.

At the same time he knew that he was able to make this close contact endurable only by carefully directing his thoughts and actions—like the trick he had acquired of never quite looking at her directly. And he was buoyed up a little by his hope that her present condition was only temporary. But if had once let himself start to think what it would mean to live a lifetime, to share bed and board, with that coldness, that inner blackness, that vacancy. . . .

Other people noticed the difference, all right. Like those crowds he had to push through in New York yesterday. Somehow people always edged away, so they wouldn't have to touch her, and he caught more than one following glance, poised between curiosity and fear. And when that other woman started to scream—lucky they had been able to lose themselves in the crowd.

The brief stopover at New York had given him time for some vitally necessary thinking. But he had been glad last night when it was over. The Pullman compartment seemed a haven of privacy.

What was it those other people noticed? True, if you looked closely, the heavy cosmetics only provided a grotesque and garish contrast to the underlying pallor, and powder did not wholly conceal the ugly dark bruise around the mouth. But the veil helped, and you had to look very closely—the cosmetics were practically a theatrical make-up. Was it her walk that they noticed, or the way her clothes hung. Her clothes always looked a little like a scarecrow's now, though you could not tell the reason. Or was there actually something to what the Bayport girl had said?

It occurred to him that he was letting his mind wander because he didn't want to get on with the distasteful task he had set himself, this task that was abhorrent to him because it was so false—or because it was so true.

"Magic is a practical science," he began quickly. He talked to the wall, as if dictating. "There is all the difference in the world between a formula in physics and a formula in magic, although they have the same name. The former describes, in terse mathematical symbols, cause-effect relationship of wide generality. But a formula in magic is a way of getting or accomplishing something. It always takes into account the motivation or desire of the person invoking the formula—be it greed, love, revenge, or what not. Whereas the experiment in physics is essentially independent of the experimenter. In short, there has been little or no pure magic, comparable to pure science.

"This distinction between physics and magic is only an accident of history. Physics started out as a kind of magic, too—witness alchemy and the mystical mathematics of Pythagoras. And modern physics is ultimately as practical as magic, but it possesses a superstructure of theory that magic lacks. Magic could be given such a superstructure by research in pure magic and by the investigation and correlation of the magic formulas of different peoples and times, with a view to deriving basic formulas which could be expressed in mathematical symbols and which would have a wide application. Most persons practicing magic have been too interested in immediate results to bother about theory. But just as research in pure science has ultimately led, seemingly by accident, to results of vast practical importance, so research in pure magic might be expected to yield similar results.

"The work of Rhine at Duke, indeed, has been very close to pure magic, with its piling up of evidence for clairvoyance, prophecy, and telepathy; its investigation of the direct linkage between all minds, their ability to affect each other instantaneously, even when they are on opposite sides of the earth."

He waited a moment, then went on.

"The subject matter of magic is akin to that of physics, in that it deals with certain forces and materials, though these—"

"I believe it is more akin to psychology," the voice interrupted.

"How so?" He still looked at the wall.

"Because it concerns the control of other beings, the summoning of them, and the constraining of them to perform certain actions."

"Good. That is very suggestive. Fortunately, formulas

may still hold good so long as their reference is clear, though we are ignorant of the precise nature of the entities to which they refer. For example, a physicist need not be able to give a visual description of an atom, even if the term visual appearance has any meaning when applied to an atom, which is doubtful. Similarly, a sorcerer need not be able to describe the appearance and nature of the entity he summons—hence the common references in the literature of magic to indescribable and nameless horrors. But the point is well taken. Many seemingly impersonal forces, when broken down sufficiently, become something very much like personality. It's not too far-fetched to say that it would take a science resembling psychology to describe the behavior of a single electron, with all its whims and impulses, though electrons in the aggregate obey relatively simple laws, just as human beings do when considered as crowds. The same holds true of the basic entities of magic, and to a much greater degree.

"It is partly for this reason that magical processes are so unreliable and dangerous, and why their working can be so readily impeded if the intended victim is on guard against them—as your formulas have to our knowledge been nullified since Mrs. Gunnison stole your notebook."

His words possessed for him an incredibly strange overtone. But it was only by maintaining a dry, scholarly manner that he could keep going. He knew that if he permitted himself to be casual, mental confusion would engulf him.

"There remains one all-important consideration," he went on swiftly. "Magic appears to be a science which markedly depends on its environment—that is, the situation of the world and the general conditions of the cosmos at any particular time. For example, Euclidean geometry is useful on Earth, but out in the great depths of space a non-Euclidean geometry is more practical. The same is true of magic, but to a more striking degree. The basic, unstated formulas of magic appear to change with the passage of time, requiring frequent restatement—though it might conceivably be possible to discover master-formulas governing that change. It has been speculated that the laws of physics show a similar evolutionary tendency—though if they do evolve, it is at a much less rapid rate than those of magic. For example, it is believed that the speed of light may slowly change with its age. It is natural that the laws of magic should evolve more swiftly, since magic depends on a contact between the material world and another level of being—and that contact is complex and may be shifting rapidly.

"Take astrology, for example. In the course of several thousand years, the precession of equinoxes has put the Sun into entirely different celestial houses—signs of the Zodiac—at the same times of year. A person born, say, on March 22nd, is still said to be born in Aries, though he is actually born when the Sun is in the constellation Pisces. A failure to take into consideration this change since the formulas of astrology were first discovered, has rendered the formulas obsolete and invalidated them for—"

"It is my belief," the voice broke in, like a phonograph suddenly starting, "that astrology has always been largely invalid. That it is one of the many pretended sciences which have been confused with true magic and used as a kind of window dressing. Such is my belief."

"I presume that may be the case, and it would help to explain why magic itself has been outwardly discredited as a science—which is the point I am getting at.

"Suppose the basic formula of physics—such as Newton's three laws of motion—had changed several times in the last few thousand years. The discovery of any physical laws at any time would have been vastly difficult. The same experiments would give different results in different ages. But that is the case with magic, and explains why magic has been periodically discredited and become repugnant to the rational mind. It's like what old Carr was saying about the run of cards at bridge. After a few shuffles of a multitude of cosmic factors, the laws of magic change. A sharp eye can spot the changes, but continual experimentation, of the trial-and-error sort, is necessary to keep the crude practical formulas of magic in anything like working order, especially since the basic formulas and the master-formulas have never been discovered.

"Take a concrete example—the formula I used Sunday night. It shows signs of recent revision. For instance, what did the original, unrevised formula have in place of the phonograph needle?"

"A willow whistle of a certain shape, which had been blown only once," the voice told him.

"And the platinum or iridium?"

"The original formula mentioned silver, but a heavier metal serves better. Lead, however, proved altogether ineffective. I tried it once. It was apparently too unlike silver in other respects."

"Precisely. Trial-and-error experimentation. Moreover, in the absence of thorough investigation, we cannot be sure that all the ingredients of a magic formula are essential in making it work. A comparison of the magic formulas of different countries and peoples would be helpful in this respect. It would show which ingredients are common to all formulas and therefore presumably essential, and which are not essential."

There was a discreet knock at the door. Norman spoke a few words, and the figure drew down its veil and turned toward the window, as if staring stolidly at the passing fields. Then he opened the door.

It was lunch, as long in coming as breakfast had been. And there was a new face—coffee-colored instead of ebony. Evidently the first waiter, who had shown growing nervousness in his previous trips to the compartment, had decided to let someone else get the big tip.

With a mixture of curiosity and impatience, Norman waited for the reactions of the newcomer. He was able to predict most of them. First a very quick inquisitive glance past him at the seated figure—Norman guessed they had become the major mystery of the train. Then a longer, sideways glance while setting up the folding table, ending with the eyes getting very wide; he could almost feel the coffee-colored flesh crawl. Only hurried, almost unwilling glances after that, with a growing uneasiness manifested in clumsy handling of the dishes and glassware. Then a too-pleasant smile and a hasty departure.

Only once Norman interfered—to place the knives and forks so they lay at right angles to their usual position.

The meal was a very simple one, almost ascetic. He did not look across the table as he ate. There was something worse than animal greediness about that methodical feeding. After the meal he settled back and started to light a cigarette, but—"Aren't you forgetting something?" the figure said. The question was uninfected.

He roused himself, got up and put the left-overs into a small cardboard box, covered them with a napkin he had used to wipe the dishes clean, and placed the box in his suitcase beside an envelope containing clippings from his own fingernails. The sight of the clean breakfast dishes had been one of the things which had helped to disturb the first waiter, but Norman was determined to adhere strictly to all taboos that Tansy seemed to desire.

So he collected food fragments, saw to it that no knives or other sharp instruments pointed toward himself or his companion, had them sleep with their heads nearest the engine and their destination, and enforced a number of other minor regulations. Eating in private satisfied still another taboo, but there was more than one reason for that.

He glanced at his watch. Only half an hour until Hempnell. He had not realized they were so close. There was the faint sense of an almost physical resistance from the region ahead, as if the air were thickening. And his mind was tossing with a multitude of problems yet to be considered.

Deliberately turning his back, he said, "According to the myths, souls may be imprisoned in all sorts of ways—in boxes, in knots, in animals, in stones. Have you any ideas on this subject?"

As he feared, this particular question brought the usual

response. The answering words had the same dull insistence
as when he had first heard them.

"I want my soul."

His hands, clasped in his lap, tightened. This was why he
had avoided the question until now. Yet he had to know
more, if that were possible.

"But where exactly should we look for it?"

"I want my soul."

"Yes." It was hard for him to control his voice. "But
how, precisely, might it be hidden? It would help if I knew."

There was rather a long pause. Then, in robot-
imitativeness of his lecture manner: "The environment of the
soul is the human brain. If it is free, it immediately seeks such
an environment. It may be said that soul and body are two
separate creatures, living together in a symbiotic relationship
so intimate and tight that they normally seem to be only one
creature. The closeness of this contact appears to have in-
creased with the centuries. Indeed, when the body it is
occupying dies, the soul is usually unable to escape and
appears to die too. But by supernatural means the soul may
sometimes be divorced from the body it is occupying. Then,
if it is prevented from re-entering its own body, it is irresistibly drawn to another, whether or not that other body possesses a soul. And so the captive soul is usually imprisoned in
the brain of its captor and forced to view and feel, in complete
intimacy, the workings of that soul. Therein lies perhaps its
chief torment."

Beads of sweat prickled Norman's scalp and forehead.

His voice did not shake, but it was unnaturally heavy and
sibilant as he asked, "What is Evelyn Sawtelle like?"

The answer sounded as if it were being read verbatim from
the summary of a political dossier.

"She is dominated by a desire for social prestige. She
spends most of her time in unsuccessfully attempting to be
snobbish. She has romantic ideas about herself, but since
they are too high-flown for any reasonable chance of satisfaction, she is prim and moralistic, with rigid standards of

conduct. She believes she was cheated in her husband, and is always apprehensive that he will lose what ground she has gained for him. Being unsure of herself, she is given to acts of maliciousness and sudden cruelty. At present she is very frightened and constantly on guard. This is why she had her magic all ready when she received the telephone call.''

Norman asked, ''Mrs. Gunnison—what do you think of her?''

''She is a woman of abundant vigor and appetites. She is a good housewife and hostess, but those activities hardly take the edge off her energies. She should have been mistress of a feudal domain. She is a born tyrant and grows fat on it. Her appetites, many of them incapable of open satisfaction in our present society, nevertheless find devious outlets. Servant girls of the Gunnisons have told stories, but not often, and then guardedly, for she is ruthless against those who are disloyal to her or threaten her security.''

''And Mrs. Carr?''

''Little can be said of her. She is conventional, an indulgent ruler of her husband, and enjoys being thought sweet and saintly. Yet she hungers for youth. It is my belief that she became a witch in middle age and therefore feels a deep frustration. I am uncertain of her deeper motivations. Curiously little of her mind shows above the surface.''

Norman nodded. Then he nerved himself. ''What,'' he asked quickly, ''do you know of the formulas for regaining a stolen soul?''

''Very little. I had a large number of such formulas jotted down in the notebook Mrs. Gunnison stole. I had the shadowy idea of working out a safeguard against some possible attack. But I do not remember them and I doubt if any of them would work. I have never tried them, and in my experience formulas never work at the first attempt. They must always be refined by trial and error.''

''But if it were possible to compare them, to find the master formula underlying them all, then—?''

''Perhaps.''

There was a knock. It was the porter come for the bags.

"Be in Hempnell in five minutes, sir. Shall I brush you in the corridor?"

Norman tipped him, but declined the service. He also told him they would carry their own bags. The porter smiled jerkily and backed out.

Norman crossed to the window. For a moment there was only the giddily-whirring gravel wall of a gully and dark trees flashing indistinctly above. But then the gravel wall gave way to a wide panorama, as the tracks swung around and down the hillside.

There was more woodland than field in the valley. The trees seemed to encrouch on the town, dwarfing it. From this particular point it looked quite tiny. But the college buildings stood out with a cold distinctness. He fancied he could make out the window of his office.

Those cold gray towers and darker roofs were like an intrusion from some other, older world, and his heart began to pound, as if he had suddenly sighted the fortress of the enemy.

CHAPTER XVII

SUPPRESSING THE IMPULSE to slink, Norman rounded the corner of Morton, squared his shoulders, and forced himself to look across the campus. The thing that hit him hardest was simply the air of normality. True, he had not consciously expected Hempnell to manifest any physical stench of evil, any outward sign of poisonous inward neurosis—or whatever it was he was battling. But this abnormal, story-book wholesomeness—the little swarms of students trooping back to the dormitories and over to the soda fountain at Student Union, the file of girls in white bound for a tennis lesson, the friendly familiar look of the wide walks—it struck at the very core of his mind, as if deliberately trying to convict him of insanity.

"Don't fool yourself," his thoughts told him. "Some of those laughing girls are already infected, with something. Their very respectable mammas have given them delicate hints about all sorts of unusual ways of Making Wishes Work. They already know that there's more to neurosis than the psychiatry books tell and that the economics texts don't even scratch the surface of the Magic of Money. And it

certainly isn't chemistry formulas they're memorizing when
that faraway look comes into their eyes as they sip their cokes
or chatter about their boy friends.''

He turned into Morton and quickly mounted the stairs.

His capacity for surprise was not yet exhausted, however,
as he realized when he saw a group of students emerging
from the classroom at the other end of the third-floor corridor. He glanced at his watch and realized that it was one of
his own classes dispersing after having waited ten minutes—
the usual tardy professor's grace—for him to appear. That
was right, he reminded himself, he was Professor Saylor, a
man with classes, committee meetings, and appointments.
He slipped around the bend in the corridor before he was
noticed.

After standing in front of the door for a few minutes, he
entered his office. Nothing seemed to have been disturbed,
but he was careful in his movements and on the alert for
unfamiliar objects. He did not put his hand into any drawer
without closely inspecting it first.

One letter in the little pile of accumulated mail was important. It was from Pollard's office, ominously requesting him
to appear at a meeting of the trustees later that week. He
smiled with grim satisfaction at this evidence that his career
was still skidding downhill.

He methodically removed certain sections from his files,
stuffed his briefcases full, and made a package of the remain-
der.

After a last glance around, during which he noted that the
Estrey dragon had not been restored to whatever had been its
original position on the roof, he started downstairs.

Outside he met Mrs. Gunnison.

He was acutely conscious of the way his arms were en-
cumbered. For a moment he did not seem able to see the
woman clearly.

''Lucky I found you,'' she began immediately. ''Harold's
been trying every which way to get in touch with you. Where
have you been?''

Suddenly she registered on him as her old, blunt, sloppy self. With a sense of mingled frustration and relief, he realized that the warfare in which he was engaged was a strictly undercover affair, and that outwardly all relationships were the same as ever. He found himself explaining how Tansy and he, week-ending with friends out in the country, had gotten a touch of food poisoning, and how his message to Hempnell must have gone astray. This lie, planned some time ago, had the advantage of providing a reason for Tansy's appearance if anyone should see her, and it would enable him to plead a recurrence of the attack as an excuse for neglecting his academic duties.

He did not expect Mrs. Gunnison to believe the lie, still he ought to be consistent.

She accepted the story without comment, offered her sympathies and went on to say, "But be sure and get in touch with Harold. I believe it has to do with that meeting of the trustees you've been asked to attend. You know, Harold thinks a great deal of you. Good-by."

He watched her puzzledly as she tramped off. Odd, but at the last moment he fancied he caught a note of genuine friendliness in her manner, as if for a moment something that was not Mrs. Gunnison had appealed to him out of her eyes.

But there was work to do. Off campus, he hurried down a side street to where his car was parked. With hardly a sidewise glance at the motionless figure in the front seat, he stepped in and drove to Sawtelle's.

The house was bigger than they needed, and the front lawn was very formal. But the grass was yellow in patches, and the soldierlike rows of flowers looked neglected.

"Wait here," he said. "Don't get out of the car under any circumstances."

To his surprise, Hervey met him at the door. There were circles under Hervey's always-worried eyes, and his fidgetiness was more than usually apparent.

"I'm so glad you've come," he said pulling Norman inside. "I don't know what I'm going to do with all these departmental responsibilities on my shoulders. Classes having to be dismissed. Stopgap instructors to be obtained. And the deadline on next year's catalogue tomorrow! Here, come into my study.'' And he pushed Norman through a huge living room, expensively but stiffly furnished, into a dingy, book-lined cubby-hole with one small window.

''I'm almost going out of my mind. I haven't dared stir out of the house since Evelyn was attacked Saturday night.''

''What!''

''Haven't you heard?'' He stopped and looked at Norman in surprise. Even here he had been trying to pace up and down, although there was not room enough. ''Why, it was in the papers. I wondered why you didn't come over or call up. I kept trying to get you at your home and the office, but no one could locate you. Evelyn's been in bed since Sunday, and she gets hysterical if I even speak of going out of the house. Just now she's asleep, thank heavens.''

Hastily Norman related his trumped-up excuse. He wanted to get back to what had happened Saturday night. As he glibly mouthed his lie about food poisoning, his mind jumped to Bayport and the telephone call to Evelyn Sawtelle that had occurred late on that same Saturday night. Only then Evelyn had seemed to be attacking, not attacked. He had come here to confront her. But now—

''Just my luck!'' Sawtelle exclaimed tragically when Norman had finished. ''The whole department falling apart the very first week I'm in charge of it—not that it's your fault of course. And young Stackpole laid up with the 'flu'.''

''We'll manage,'' said Norman. ''Sit down and tell me about Evelyn.''

Unwillingly, Sawtelle cleared a space so he could perch on the cluttered desk. He groaned when his eyes chanced to light on papers presumably concerned with urgent business.

''It happened about four o'clock Sunday morning,'' he began, aimlessly fiddling with the papers. ''I was awakened by a terrible scream. Evelyn's bed was empty. It was pitch dark out in the hall. But I could hear some sort of struggle going on downstairs. A bumping and threshing around—''

Suddenly he jerked up his head. ''What was that? I thought I heard footsteps out in the front hall.'' Before Norman could say anything he went on. ''Oh, it's just my nerves. They've been acting up ever since.

''Well, I picked up something—a vase—and went downstairs. About that time the sounds stopped. I switched on the lights and went through all the rooms. In the sewing room I found Evelyn stretched unconscious on the floor with some ghastly bruises beginning to show around her neck and mouth. Beside her lay the phone—we have it there because Evelyn has so many occasions to use it. I nearly went frantic. I called a doctor and the police. When Evelyn regained consciousness, she was able to tell us about it, although she was terribly shaken up. It seems the phone had rung. She went downstairs in the dark without waking me. Just as she was picking up the phone, a man jumped out of the corner and attacked her. She fought him off—oh, it drives me mad to think of it!—but he overpowered her and choked her unconscious.''

In his excitement Sawtelle crumpled a paper he was holding, saw what he had done, and hastily smoothed it out.

''Thank heavens I came downstairs when I did! That must have been what frightened him off. The doctor found that, except for bruises, there weren't any other injuries. Even the doctor was shocked at those bruises, though. He said he had never seen any quite like them.

''The police think that after the man got in the house he called Central and asked them to ring this phone—pretending he thought the bell was out of order or something—in order to lure someone downstairs. They were puzzled as to how he got inside, though, for all the windows and doors were shut fast. Probably I forgot to lock the front door when we went to bed—one of my pieces of unforgivable carelessness!

''The police think he was a burglar or sex offender, but I believe he must have been a real madman besides. Because there was a silver plate on the floor, and two of our silver forks jammed together strangely, and other odds and ends. And he must have been playing the phonograph in the sewing room, because it was open and the turn table was going and on the floor was one of Evelyn's speech records, smashed to bits.''

Norman stared at his jittery departmental superior, but behind the stupidity of his gaze, his thoughts were working wildly. The first idea that stayed with him was that here was physical confirmation that he had heard a bull-roarer over the Bayport phone—what else could the smashed record mean?—and that Evelyn Sawtelle was going through the motions or practicing magic as much as Tansy ever had— else what was the significance of silver plate and forks and "other odds and ends"? Also, Evelyn must have been expecting a call and been prepared for it, else why would she have had the things ready?

But then his thoughts scurried on to what Sawtelle had said about his wife's injuries—those bruises that sounded identical with the ones Tansy had inflicted on herself with, or somehow received from, a phone. The same bruises, the same possible instruments, suggested a shadow world in which black magic, thwarted, returned on its sender, or in which schemes to frighten by the pretense of black magic struck back at the guilty and psychotic mind of their originator.

"It's all my fault," Sawtelle was repeating mournfully, tugging at his necktie. Norman remembered that Sawtelle always assumed that he was guilty whenever anything hurt or merely upset Evelyn. "I should have awakened! I should have been the one to go down to the phone. When I think of that delicate creature feeling her way through the dark, and lurking just ahead of her that—Oh, and the department! I tell you I am going out of my mind. Poor Evelyn has been in such a pitifully frightened state ever since, you wouldn't believe it!'' And he tugged at his necktie so strongly that it started to choke him and he had to undo it quickly.

"I tell you, I haven't slept a wink,'' he continued when he

got his breath. "If Mrs. Gunnison hadn't been kind enough to spend a couple of hours with Evelyn yesterday morning, I don't know how I'd have managed. Even then she was too frightened to let me stir. . . . My God! . . . Evelyn!"

But Norman couldn't identify the agonized scream, and he seriously doubted whether Sawtelle could, except that it had come from the upper part of the house. Crying out, "I knew I heard footsteps! He's come back!" Sawtelle ran full tilt out of the study. Norman was just behind him, suddenly conscious of a very different fear. It was confirmed by a glance through the living-room window at his empty car.

He beat Sawtelle up the stairs and was the first to reach the bedroom door. He stopped. Sawtelle, almost gibbering with anxiety and guilt, ran into him.

It was not at all what Norman expected.

The pink silk coverlet clutched around her, Evelyn Sawtelle had retreated to the side of the bed nearest the wall. Her teeth were chattering, her face was a dirty white.

Beside the bed stood Tansy. For a moment Norman felt a great, sudden hope. Then he saw her eyes, and the hope shot away with sickening swiftness. She was not wearing the veil. In that heavy make-up with those rouged cheeks and thickly carmined lips, she looked like some indecently daubed statue, impossibly grotesque against a background of ridiculous pink silk hangings. But a hungry statue.

Sawtelle scrambled past him, shouting, "What's happened? What's happened?" He saw Tansy. "I didn't know you were here. When did you come in?" Then, "You frightened her!"

The statue spoke, and its quiet accents hushed him.

"Oh, no, I didn't frighten her. Did I, Evelyn?"

Evelyn Sawtelle was staring at Tansy in abject, wide-eyed terror, and her jaw was still working. But when she spoke, it was to say, "No, Tansy didn't . . . frighten me. We were talking together . . . and then . . . I . . . I thought I heard a noise."

"Just a noise, dear?" Sawtelle said.

"Yes . . . like footsteps . . . very quiet footsteps in the hall." She did not take her eyes off Tansy, who nodded once when she had finished.

Norman accompanied Sawtelle on a futile but highly melodramatic search of the top floor. When they came back, Evelyn was alone.

"Tansy's gone out to the car," she told Norman weakly. "I'm sure I just imagined those footsteps."

But her eyes were still full of fear when he left her and she seemed quite unaware of her husband, although he was fussing about straightening the coverlet and shaking out the pillows.

Tansy was sitting in the car, staring ahead. Norman could see the body was still dominated by its one emotion. He had to ask a question.

"She does not have my soul," was the answer. "I questioned her at length. As a final and certain test I embraced her. That was when she screamed. She is very much afraid of the dead."

"What did she tell you?"

"She said that someone came and took my soul from her. Someone who did not trust her very much. Someone who desired my soul, to keep as a hostage and for other reasons. Mrs. Gunnison."

The knuckles of Norman's hands were white on the steering wheel. He was thinking of that puzzling look of appeal that Mrs. Gunnison had given him.

CHAPTER XVIII

PROFESSOR CARR'S OFFICE seemed an attempt to reduce the lusty material world to the virginal purity of geometry. The narrow walls displayed three framed prints of conic sections. Atop the bookcase filled with slim, gold-stamped mathematical books, were two models of complex curved surfaces executed in German silver and fine wire. The half-furled umbrella in the corner might have been another such model. And the surface of the small desk between Carr himself and Norman was bare except for five sheets of paper covered with symbols. Carr's thin, pale finger touched the top sheet.

"Yes," he said, "these are allowable equations in symbolic logic."

Norman had been pretty sure they were, but he was glad to hear a mathematician say so. The hurried reference he had made to *Principia Mathematica* had not altogether satisfied him.

"The capitals stand for classes of entities, the lower case letters for relationships," he said helpfully.

"Ah, yes." Carr tugged at the dark skin of his chin beneath the white Vandyke. "But what sort of entities and relationships are they?"

"You could perform operations on the equations, couldn't you, without knowing the reference of the individual symbols?" Norman countered.

"Most certainly. And the results of the operations would be valid whether the entities referred to were apples, battleships, poetic ideas, or signs of the zodiac. Always providing, of course, that the original references between entity and symbol had been made correctly."

"Then here's my problem," Norman went on hastily. "There are seventeen equations on that first sheet. As they stand, they seem to differ a great deal. Now I'm wondering if one simple, underlying equation doesn't appear in each of the seventeen, jumbled up with a lot of nonessential terms and procedures. Each of the other sheets presents a similar problem."

"Hm-m-m—" Professor Carr began to finger a pencil, and his eyes started to go back to the first sheet, but he checked the movement. "I must confess I'm rather curious about the entities referred to," he said, and added innocently, "I wasn't aware that there had been attempts to apply symbolic logic to sociology."

Norman was prepared for this. "I'll be frank with you, Linthicum," he said. "I have a pretty wild, off-trail theory, and I've promised myself I won't discuss it until I have a better idea of whether or not there's anything to it."

Carr's face broke into a reminiscent smile. "I think I understand your sentiments," he said. "I can still recall the disastrous consequences of my announcement that I had trisected the angle.

"Of course, I was only in seventh grade at the time," he added hastily.

"Though I did give my teacher a bad half-hour," he finished with a touch of pride.

When he next spoke, it was with a return to his mood of boyishly sly curiosity. "Nevertheless, I'm very much piqued by those symbols. As it stands they might refer to . . . hm-m-m . . . anything."

"I'm sorry," said Norman. "I know I'm asking a lot of you."

"Not at all. Not at all." Twiddling the pencil Carr glanced again at the sheet. Something caught his eye. "Hm-m-m . . . this is very interesting," he said. "I hadn't noticed this before." And his pencil began to fly about the sheet, deftly striking out terms, neatly inscribing new equations. The single vertical furrow between his gray eyebrows deepened. In a moment he was wholly absorbed.

With an unbreathed sigh of relief, Norman leaned back. He felt dog-tired, and his eyes hurt. Those five sheets represented twenty hours of uninterrupted work. Tuesday night, Wednesday morning, part of Wednesday afternoon. Even at that he couldn't have done it without Tansy to take notes from his dictation. He had come to trust absolutely her present mindless, machinelike accuracy.

Half hypnotized, he watched the agile old fingers half fill a fresh sheet of paper with derived equations. Their swift, orderly movements intensified the serene, monastic quiet of the small office.

What strangeness pressing on the heels of strangeness it was, Norman thought dreamily, not only to pretend to believe in black magic in order to overawe three superstitious, psychotic women who had a hold on his wife's mental life, but even to invoke the modern science of symbolic logic in the service of that pretended belief. Symbolic logic used to disentangle the contradictions and ambiguities of witchcraft formulas! What wouldn't old Carr say if he were really told "the entities referred to"!

And yet it had only been by invoking the superior prestige of higher mathematics that he had been able to convince Tansy that he could make strong enough magic to work against her enemies. And that was all in the best traditions of sorcery, when you came to think of it. Sorcerers always tried to incorporate the latest bits of information and wisdom into their systems, for prestige purposes. What was sorcery but a battle for prestige in the realms of mysticism, and what was a

sorcerer but someone who had gotten an illegitimate mental
jump on his fellows?

What a ludicrous picture it was, though (everything was
beginning to seem hysterically laughable to his weary mind):
a woman who half believed in witchcraft driven mad by three
women who perhaps believed fully in witchcraft or perhaps
not at all, their schemes opposed by a husband who believed
not at all, but pretended to believe to the full—and was
determined to act in every way in accord with that belief.

Or, he thought (his dreaminess verging toward slumber
and the sweet mathematical simplicity of his surroundings
wooing his mind toward visions of absolute space in which
infinity was before his eyes), why not drop all these stuffy
rationalizations and admit that Tansy had something called a
soul and that it had been stolen by the thin witch Evelyn
Sawtelle, and then stolen from her by the fat witch Hulda
Gunnison, and that he was even now seeking the magic that
would—

He jerked himself resolutely awake and back to the world
of rationalizations again. Carr had shoved a paper toward
him and had immediately started to work on another of the
five sheets Norman had given him.

"You've already found the first underlying equations?"
Norman asked incredulously.

Carr seemed annoyed at the interruption. "Surely. Of
course." His pencil had already started to dart about again,
when he stopped and looked at Norman oddly. "Yes," he
said, "It's the last equation there, the short one. To tell the
truth, I wasn't sure I'd find one when I started, but your
entities and relationships seem to have some sense to them,
whatever they are." And then he and his pencil were off
again.

Norman shivered, staring at the brief ultimate equation,
wondering what its meaning might be. He could not tell
without referring to his code and he certainly didn't want to
get that out here.

"Sorry to be making all this work for you," he said dully.

Carr spared him a glance. "Not at all, I enjoy it. I always did have a peculiar knack for these things."

The afternoon shadows deepened. Norman switched on the overhead light, and Carr thanked him with a quick preoccupied nod. The pencil flew. Three more sheets had been shoved across to Norman, and Carr was finishing the last one, when the door opened.

"Linthicum!" came the sweet voice, with hardly a trace of reproachfulness. "Whatever's keeping you? I've waited downstairs half an hour."

"I'm sorry, dear," said the old man, looking at his watch and his wife. "But I had become so absorbed—"

She saw Norman. "Oh, I didn't know you had a visitor. *Whatever* will Professor Saylor *think!* I'm afraid I've given him the impression that I tyrannize over you."

And she accompanied the words with such a quaint smile that Norman found himself echoing Carr's "Not at all."

"Professor Saylor looks *dead* tired," she said, peering at Norman anxiously. "I hope you haven't been wearing him out, Linthicum."

"Oh, no, my dear, I've been doing all the work," her husband told her.

She walked around the desk and looked over his shoulder. "What is it?" she asked, pleasantly.

"I don't know," he said. He straightened up and, winking at Norman, went on, "I believe that, behind these symbols, Professor Saylor is revolutionizing the science of sociology. But it's a great secret. And in any case I haven't the slightest idea of what the symbols refer to. I'm just being a sort of electronic brain."

With a polite, by-your-leave nod toward Norman, Mrs. Carr picked up one of the sheets and studied it through her thick glasses. But apparently at sight of the massed rows of symbols, she put it down.

"Mathematics is not my forte," she explained. "I was *such* a poor scholar."

"Nonsense, Flora," said Carr. "Whenever we go to the

market, you're much quicker at totaling the bill than I am. And I try to beat you, too."

"But that's such a *little* thing," said Mrs. Carr delightedly.

"I'll only be a moment more," said her husband, returning to his calculations.

Mrs. Carr spoke across to Norman in a half-whisper. "Oh, Professor Saylor, would you be so kind as to convey a message to Tansy? I want to invite her for bridge tomorrow night—that's Thursday—with Hulda Gunnison and Evelyn Sawtelle. Linthicum has a *meeting*."

"I'll be glad to," said Norman quickly. "But I'm afraid she might not be up to it." And he explained about the food poisoning.

"How too, too *terrible!*" observed Mrs. Carr. "Couldn't I come over and help her?"

"Thank you," Norman lied, "but we have someone staying with her."

"How *wise*," said Mrs. Carr, and she looked at Norman intently, as if to spy out the source of that wisdom. Her steady gaze made him feel uncomfortable, it seemed at once so predatory and so naive. It somehow wouldn't have surprised him in one of his students, one of his girl students, but in this old woman—

Carr put down his pencil. "There," he said. "I'm done."

With further expression of thanks, Norman gathered up the sheets.

"Really no trouble at all," Carr assured him. "You gave me a very exciting afternoon. I must confess you've aroused my curiosity."

"Linithicum dotes on anything mathematical, especially when it's like a puzzle," Mrs. Carr told him. "Why, once," she continued, with a kind of roguish indulgence, "he made all sorts of tabulation on *horse races*."

"Er . . . yes . . . but only as a concrete example of the calculus of probabilities," Carr interposed quickly. But his smile was equally indulgent.

Her hand was on his shoulder, and he had reached up his own to cover hers. Frail, yet somehow hearty, withered, yet somehow fresh, they seemed like the perfect aged couple.

"I promise you," Norman told him, "that if I revolutionize the science of sociology, you'll be the first to hear of it. Good evening." And he bowed out.

As soon as he could hurry home he got out the code. "W" was the identifying letter at the top of the first sheet. He thought he remembered what that meant, but he looked it up just to be sure.

"W—To conjure out the soul."

Yes, that was it. He turned to the supplementary sheet covered with Carr's calculations, and carefully decoded the final equation. "C—Notched strip of copper." He nodded. "T—Twirl sunwise." He frowned. He could have expected that to cancel out. Good thing he'd gotten a mathematician's help in simplifying the seventeen equations, each representing a different people's formula for conjuring out the soul—Arabian, Zulu, Polynesian, American Negro, American Indian, and so on; the most recent formulas available, and ones that had known actual use.

"A—Deadly amanita." Bother! He'd been certain that one would cancel out. It would be a bit of time and trouble getting a deathcup mushroom. Well, he could manage without that formula if he had to. He took up two other sheets: "V—To control the soul of another," "Z—To cause the dwellers in a house to sleep" and set to work on one of them. In a few minutes he had assured himself that the ingredients presented no special difficulties, save that Z required a Hand of Glory to be used as well as graveyard dirt to be thrown onto the roof of the house in which sleep was to be enforced. But he ought to have little difficulty in filching a suitable severed hand from the anatomy lab. And then if—

Conscious of a sudden weariness and of a revulsion from these formulas, which persisted in seeming more obscene than ridiculous, he pushed back his chair. For the first time since had had come into the house, he looked at the figure by the window. It sat in the rocking chair, face turned toward the drawn curtains. When it started rocking, he did not know. But the muscles of its body automatically continued the rhythmical movement, once it had begun.

With the suddenness of a blow, longing for Tansy struck him. Her intonations, her gestures, her mannerisms, her funny fancies—all the little things that go to make a person real and human and loved—he wanted them all instantly; and the presence of this dead-alive imitation, this husk of Tansy, only made the longing less bearable. And what sort of a man was he, to be puttering around with occult formulas, while all the time—"There are things that can be done to a soul," she had said. "Servant girls of the Gunnisons have told stories—" He ought to go straight to the Gunnisons, confront Hulda, and force the issue!

With a quick effort he subdued his anger. Any such action on his part might ruin everything. How could you use open force against someone who held the mentality, the very consciousness, of your dearest possession as a hostage? No, he had been all over this before and his course was set. He might fight those women with their own weapons; these repugnant occult formulas were his best hope and he had gotten his usual punishment for making the mistake of looking at its face. Deliberately he moved to the other side of the table, so his back was toward the rocking chair.

But he was restless, his muscles itching with fatigue poisons, and for the moment he could not get back to work.

Suddenly he spoke. "Why do you suppose everything has become violent and deadly so abruptly?"

"The Balance was upset," was the answer. There was no interruption in the steady rocking.

"How was that?" He started to look over the back of his chair, but checked himself in time.

"It happened when I ceased to practice magic." The rocking was a grating monotony.

"But why should that lead to violence?"

"It upset the Balance."

"Yes, but how can that explain the abruptness of the shift from relatively trivial attacks to a deadly maliciousness?"

The rocking had stopped. There was no answer. But, as he told himself, he knew the answer already that was shaping in that mindless mind behind him. This witches' warfare it believed in was very much like trench warfare or a battle between fortified lines—a state of siege. Just as reinforced concrete or armor plating nullified the shells, so counter-charms and protective procedures rendered relatively futile the most violent onslaughts. But once the armor and concrete were gone, and the witch who had foresworn witchcraft was out in a kind of no man's land—

Then, too, fear of the savage counterattacks that could be launched from such highly fortified positions, was a potent factor in discouraging direct assaults. The natural thing would be to sit pat, snipe away, and only attack if the enemy exposed himself recklessly. Besides, there were probably all sorts of unsuspected hostages and secret agreements, all putting a damper on violence.

This idea also seemed to explain why Tansy's apparently pacific action had upset the Balance. What would any country think, if in the midst of a war, its enemy scuttled all his battleships and dismantled all his aircraft, apparently laying himself wide open to attack? For the realistic mind, there could be only one likely answer. Namely, that the enemy had discovered a weapon far more potent than battleships or aircraft, and was planning to ask for a peace that would turn out to be a trap. The only thing would be to strike instantly and hard, before the secret weapon could be brought into play.

"I think—" he started to say.

Then something—perhaps a faint *whish* in the air or a slight creaking of the floor under the heavy carpet, or some less tangible sensation—caused him to glance around.

With a writhing jerk sideways, he managed—just managed—to get his head out of the path of that descending metal flail, which was all he saw at first. With a shocking *swish* it crashed downward against the heavy back of the chair and its force was broken. But his shoulder, which took only the broken blow, went numb.

Clawing at the table with his good hand, he threw himself forward against the table and whirled around.

He recoiled from the sight as from another blow, throwing back his good hand to save himself from overbalancing.

It was poised in the center of the room, having sprung back catlike after the first blow failed. Almost stiff-legged, but with the weight forward. In stocking feet—the slippers that might have made a noise were laid by the rocking chair. In its hand was the steel poker, stealthily lifted from the stand by the fireplace.

There was life in the face now. But it was life that champed the teeth and drooled, life that pinched and flared the nostrils with every breath, life that switched hair from the eyes with quick, angry flirts, life that glared redly and steadily.

With a low snarl it lifted the poker and struck, not at him, but at the chandelier overhead. Pitch darkness flooded the room he had curtained tightly against prying eyes.

There was a rush of soft footsteps. He ducked to one side. Nevertheless, the *swish* came perilously close. There was a sound as if it had dived or rolled across the table after he eluded the headlong rush—he could hear the slur of papers skidding and the faint crackle as some drifted to the floor. Then silence, except for the rapid *snuff-snuff* of animal breathing.

He crouched on the carpet, trying not to move a muscle, straining his ears to catch the direction of that breathing. Abominable, he thought, how inefficient the human auditory system is at localizing a sound. First the snuffing sound came from one direction, then another, although he could not hear the slightest rustle of intervening movement—until he began to lose his sense of direction in the room. He tried to remember his exact movements in springing away from the table. As he had hit the carpet, he had spun around. But how far? Was he facing toward or away from the wall? In his zeal to avoid the possibility of anyone spying on them, he had blacked out this room and the bedroom, and the blackout was effective. No discernible atom of light filtered through from the night outside. He was somewhere on what was beginning to seem an endless expanse of carpet, a low-ceilinged, wall-less infinity.

And somewhere else on that expanse, it was. Could it see and hear more than he? Could it discern form in retinal patterns that were only blackness to Tansy's sane soul? What was it waiting for? He strained his ears, but the rapid breathing was no longer audible.

This might be the darkness of some jungle floor, roofed by yards of matted creepers. Civilization is a thing of light. When light goes, civilization is snuffed out. Norman was rapidly being reduced to *its* level. Perhaps it had counted on that when it smashed the lights. This might be the inner chamber of some primeval cave, and he some cloudy-minded primitive huddled in abject terror of his mate, into whose beloved form a demon had been conjured up by the witch woman—the brawny, fat witch woman with the sullen lip and brutish eyes, and copper ornaments twisted in matted red hair. Should he grope for his ax and seek to smash the demon from the skull where it was hiding? Or should he seek out the witch woman and throttle her until she called off her demon? But how could he constrain his wife meanwhile? If the tribe found her, they would slay her instantly—it was the law. And even now the demon in her was seeking to slay him.

With thoughts almost as murky and confused as those of that ghostly primitive forerunner, Norman sought to grapple with the problem, until he suddenly realized what it was waiting for.

Already his muscles were aching. He was getting twinges of pain from his shoulder as the numbness went out of it. Soon he would make an involuntary movement. And in that instant it would be upon him.

Cautiously he stretched out his hand. Slowly—very slowly—he swung it around until it touched a small table and located a large book. Clamping thumb and fingers around the book where it projected from the table edge, he lifted it and drew it to him. His muscles began to shake a little from the effort to maintain absolute quiet.

With a slow movement he launched the book toward the center of the room, so that it hit the carpet a few feet from him. The sound drew the instant response he had hoped for. Waiting a second he dove forward, seeking to pin it to the floor. But its cunning was greater than he had guessed. His arms closed on a heavy cushion that it had hurled toward the book, and only luck saved him as the poker thudded savagely against the carpet close by his head.

Clutching out blindly, his hands closed on the cold metal. There was a moment of straining as it sought to break his grip. Then he was sprawling backward, the poker in his hand, and the footsteps were retreating toward the rear of the house.

He followed it to the kitchen. A drawer, jerked out too far, fell to the floor, and he heard the chilling clatter and scrape of cutlery.

But there was enough light in the kitchen to show him its silhouette. He lunged at the upraised hand holding the long knife, caught the wrist. Then it threw itself against him, and they dropped to the floor.

He felt the warm body against his, murderously animated to the last limits of its strength. For a moment he felt the coldness of the flat of the knife against his cheek, then he had forced the weapon away. He doubled up his legs to protect himself from its knees. It surged convulsively down on him and he felt jaws clamp the arm with which he held away the knife. Teeth sawed sideways trying to penetrate the fabric of his coat. Cloth ripped as he sought with his free hand to drag the body away from him. Then he found the hair and forced back the head so the teeth lost their grip. It dropped the knife and clawed at his face. He seized the fingers seeking his eyes and nostrils; it snarled and spat at him. Steadily he forced the arms, twisting them behind it, and with a sudden effort got to his knees. Strangled sounds of fury came from its throat.

Only too keenly aware of how close his muscles were to the trembling weakness of exhaustion, he shifted his grip so that with one hand he held the straining wrists. With the other he groped sideways, jerked open the lower door of the cabinet, found a length of cord.

CHAPTER XIX

"IT'S PRETTY SERIOUS this time, Norm," said Harold Gunnison. "Fenner and Liddell really want your scalp."

Norman drew his chair closer, as if the discussion were the real reason for his visit to Gunnison's office this morning.

Gunnison went on. "I think they're planning to rake up that Margaret Van Nice business and start yelping that where there's smoke there must be fire. And they may try to use Theodore Jennings against you, Claim that his 'nervous breakdown' was aggravated by unfairness and undue severity on your part, et cetera. Of course we have the strongest defense for you in both cases, still just talking about such matters is bound to have an unfavorable effect on the other trustees. And then this talk on sex you're going to give the Off-campus Mothers, and those theatrical friends of yours you've invited to the college. I have no personal objections, Norm, but you did pick a bad time."

Norman nodded, dutifully, Mrs. Gunnison ought to be here soon. The maid had told him over the phone that she had just left for her husband's office.

"Of course, such matters aren't enough in themselves."

Gunnison looked unusually heavy-eyed and grave. "But as I say, they have a bad taste, and they can be used as an entering wedge. The real danger will come from a restrained but concerted attack on your conduct of classes, your public utterances, and perhaps even trivial details of your social life, followed by talk about the need for retrenchment where it is expeditious—you know what I mean." He paused. "What really bothers me is that Pollard's cooled toward you. I told him just what I thought of Sawtelle's appointment, but he said the trustees had overruled him. He's a good man, but he's a politician." And Gunnison shrugged, as if it were common knowledge that the distinction between politicians and professors went back to the Ice Age.

Norman roused himself. "I'm afraid I insulted him last week. We had a long talk and I blew up."

Gunnison shook his head. "That wouldn't explain it. He can absorb insults. If he sides against you, it will be because he feels it necessary or at least expeditious (I hate that word) on the grounds of public opinion. You know his way of running the college. Every couple of years he throws some-one to the wolves."

Norman hardly heard him. He was thinking of Tansy's body as he had left it—the trussed-up limbs, the lolling jaw, the hoarse heavy breathing from the whiskey he had finally made it guzzle. He was taking a long chance, but he couldn't see any other way. At one time last night he had almost decided to call a doctor and perhaps have it placed in a sanitarium. But if he did that he might lose forever his chance to restore Tansy's rightful self. What psychiatrist would believe the morbid plot he knew existed against his wife's sanity? For similar reasons there was no friend he could call on for help. No, the only way was to strike swiftly at Mrs. Gunnison. But it was not pleasant to think of such headlines as: "PROFESSOR'S WIFE A TORTURE VICTIM, FOUND TRUSSED IN CLOSET BY MATE."

"It's really serious, Norm," Gunnison was repeating. "My wife thinks so, and she's smart about these things. She knows people."

His wife! Obediently, Norman nodded.

"Hard luck it had to come to a head now," Gunnison continued, "when you've been having more than your share of troubles with sickness and what-not." Norman could see that Gunnison was looking with a faint shade of inquisitiveness at the strip of surgical tape close to the corner of his left eye and the other one just below his nostrils. But he attempted no explanation. Gunnison shifted about and re-settled himself in his chair. "Norm," he said, "I've got the feeling that something's gone wrong. Ordinarily I'd say you could weather this blow all right—you're one of our two-three best men—but I've got the feeling that something's gone wrong all the way down the line."

The offer his words conveyed was obvious enough, and Norman knew it was made in good faith. But only for a moment did he consider telling Gunnison even a fraction of the truth. It would be like taking his troubles into the law courts, and he could imagine—with the sharp, almost hallucinatory vividness of extreme fatigue—what that would be like.

Imagine putting Tansy in the witness box even in her earlier non-violent condition. "You say, Mrs. Saylor, that your soul was stolen from your body?" "Yes." "You are conscious of the absence of your soul?" "No, I'm not conscious, of anything." "Not conscious? You surely don't mean that you are unconscious?" "But I do. I can neither see nor hear." "You mean that you can neither see nor hear me?" "That is correct." "How then—" Bang of the judge's gavel. "If this tittering does not cease immediately, I will clear the court!" Or Mrs. Gunnison called to the witness box and he himself bursting out with an impassioned plea to the jury. "Gentlemen, look at her eyes! Watch them closely, I implore you. My wife's soul is there, if you would only see it!"

"What's the matter, Norm?" he heard Gunnison ask. The genuine sympathy of the voice tugged at him confusedly. Groggy with sudden sleepiness he tried to rally himself to answer.

Mrs. Gunnison walked in.

"Hullo," she said. "I'm glad you two finally got together." Almost patronizingly she looked Norman over. "I don't think you've slept for the last two nights," she announced brusquely. "And what's happened to your face? Did that cat of yours finally scratch it?"

Gunnison laughed, as he usually did, at his wife's frankness. "What a woman. Loves dogs. Hates cats. But she's right about your needing sleep, Norm."

The sight of her and the sound of her voice stung Norman into an icy wakefulness. She looked as if she had been sleeping ten hours a night for some time. An expensive green suit set off her red hair and gave her a kind of buxom beauty. Her slip showed and the coat was buttoned in a disorderly way, but now it conveyed to Norman the effect of the privileged carelessness of some all-powerful ruler who is above ordinary standards of neatness. For once she was not carrying the bulging purse. His heart leaped.

He did not trust himself to look into her eyes. He started to get up.

"Don't go yet, Norm," Gunnison told him. "There's a lot we should talk about."

"Yes, why don't you stay?" Mrs. Gunnison seconded.

"Sorry," said Norman. "I'll come around this afternoon if you can spare the time. Or tomorrow morning, at the latest."

"Be sure and do that," said Gunnison seriously. "The trustees are meeting tomorrow afternoon."

Mrs. Gunnison sat down in the chair he had vacated.

"My regards to Tansy," she said. "I'll be seeing her tonight at the Carrs'—that is, if she's recovered sufficiently." Norman nodded. Then he walked out rapidly and shut the door behind him.

While his hand was still on the knob, he saw Mrs. Gunnison's green purse lying on the table in the outer office. It was just this side of the display case of Prince Rupert drops and similar oddities. His heart jumped again.

There was one girl in the outer office—a student employee. He went to her desk.

"Miss Miller," he said, "would you be so kind as to get me the grade sheets of the following students?" And he rattled off half a dozen names.

"The sheets are in the Recorder's Office, Professor Saylor," she said, a little doubtfully.

"I know. But you tell them I sent you. Dr. Gunnison and I want to look them over."

Obediently she took down the names.

As the door closed behind her he pulled out the top drawer of her desk, where he knew the key for the display case would be.

A few minutes later Mrs. Gunnison came out.

"I thought I heard you go out," she exclaimed sharply. Then in her usual blunt manner, "Are you waiting for me to leave, so you can talk to Harold alone?"

He did not answer. He glanced at her nose.

She picked up her purse. "There's really no point in trying to make a secret of it," she said. "I know as much about your troubles here as he does—in fact, considerably more. And, to be honest, they're pretty bad." Her voice had begun to assume the arrogance of the victor. She smiled at him.

He continued to look at her nose.

"And you needn't pretend you're not worried," she went on, her voice reacting irritably to his silence. "Because I know you are. And tomorrow Pollard will ask for your resignation." Then, "What are you staring at?"

"Nothing," he answered, hastily, averting his glance.

With an incredulous sniff, she took out her mirror, glanced at it puzzledly for a moment, then held it up for a detailed inspection of her face.

To Norman the second hand of the wall clock seemed to stand still.

Very softly, but swiftly, and in a most casual voice, which did not even cause Mrs. Gunnison to look around he said, "I know you've stolen my wife's soul, Mrs. Gunnison, and I know how you've stolen it. I know a bit about stealing souls myself; for instance, if you're in a room with someone whose soul you want, and they happen to be looking into a mirror, and the mirror breaks while their reflection is still in it, then—''

With a swift, tinkling crack, not very loud, the mirror in Mrs. Gunnison's hand puffed into a little cloud of iridescent dust.

Instantly it seemed to Norman that a weight added itself to his mind, a tangible darkness pressed down upon his thoughts.

The gasp of astonishment or fear that issued from Mrs. Gunnison's lips was cut short. What seemed a loose, stupid look flowed slowly over her face, but it was only because the muscles of her face had quite relaxed.

Norman stepped up to Mrs. Gunnison and took her arm. For a moment she stared at him, emptily, then her body lurched, she took a slow step, then another, as he said, ''Come with me. It's your best chance.''

He trembled, hardly able to credit his success, as she followed him into the hall. Near the stairs they met Miss Miller returning with a handful of large cards.

''I'm very sorry to have put you to the trouble,'' he told her. ''But it turned out that we don't need them. You had better return them to the Recorder's Office.''

The girl nodded with a polite but somewhat wry smile. ''Professors!''

As Norman steered the uncharacteristically docile Mrs. Gunnison out of the Administration Building, the queer darkness still pressed upon his thoughts. It was like nothing he had ever before experienced.

Suddenly then the darkness parted, as storm clouds might part at sunset, letting through a narrow beam of crimson light. Only the storm clouds were inside his mind and the crimson light was impotent red rage and obscene anger. And yet it was not wholly unfamiliar.

From it, Norman's mind cringed. The campus ahead seemed to wobble and waver, tinged by a faint red glare.

He thought: "If there were such a thing as split personality, and if a crack appeared in the wall between those separate consciousnesses . . ."

But that was insanity.

Abruptly another memory buffeted him—words that had issued from Tansy's lips in the Pullman compartment: "The environment of the soul is the human brain."

Again: "If it is prevented from re-entering its own body, it is irresistibly drawn to another, whether or not that other body possesses a soul. And so the captive soul is usually imprisoned in the brain of its captor."

Just then, through the slit in the darkness, riding a wave in the pounding red anger that hurled it to the center of his mind, came an intelligible thought. The thought was simple, "Stupid man, how did you do it?" but it, like the red rage, was so utterly *like* Mrs. Gunnison that he accepted (whether or not it meant he was crazy, whether or not it meant witchcraft was true) that the mind of Mrs. Gunnison was inside his skull, talking with his mind.

For a moment he glanced at the slack-featured face of the hulking female body he was piloting across the campus.

For a moment he quailed at the idea of touching, with his mind, naked personality.

But only for a moment. Then (whether or not it meant he was crazy) his acceptance was complete. He walked across campus, talking inside his head with Mrs. Gunnison.

The questioning thought was repeated: "How did you do it?"

Before he realized it, his own thoughts had answered:

"It was the Prince Rupert mirror from the display case. The warmth of your fingers shattered it. I held it in the folds of my handkerchief while transferring it to your pocketbook. According to primitive belief, your reflection is your soul, or a vehicle for your soul. If a mirror breaks when your reflection is in it, your soul is trapped outside your body." All this, without the machinery of speech to delay it, flashed in an instant.

Instantly too, Mrs. Gunnison's next thought came through

the slit in the darkness. "Where are you taking my body?"

"To our house."

"What do you want?"

"My wife's soul."

There was a long pause. The slit in the darkness closed, then opened again.

"You cannot take it. I hold it, as you hold my soul. But my soul hides it from you. And my soul holds it."

"I cannot take it. But I can hold your soul until you return my wife's soul to her body."

"What if I refuse?"

"Your husband is a realist. He will not believe what your body tells him. He will consult the best alienists. He will be very much grieved. But in the end he will commit your body to an asylum."

He could sense defeat and submission—and a kind of panic, too—in the texture of the answering thought. But defeat and submission were not yet admitted directly.

"You will not be able to hold my soul. You hate it. It fills you with abhorrence. Your mind will not be able to endure it."

Then, in immediate substantiation of this statement, there came through the slit a nasty trickle growing swiftly to a spate. His chief detestations were quickly spied out and rasped upon. He began to hurry his steps, so that the mindless bulk beside him breathed hard.

"There was Ann," came Mrs. Gunnison's thoughts, not in words but in the complete fullness of memory. "Ann came to work for me eight years ago. A frail-looking little blonde, but able to get through a hard day's work for all that. She was very submissive, and a prey to fear. Do you know that it is possible to rule people through fear alone, without an atom of direct force? A sharp word, a stern look—it's the implications that do it, not what's said directly. Gradually I gathered about myself all the grim prestige that father, teacher, and preacher had had for Ann. I could make her cry by looking at her in a certain way. I could make her writhe with fright just by standing outside the door of her bedroom. I could make her hold hot dishes without a whimper while serving us at dinner, and make her wait while I talked to Harold. I've looked at her hands afterward.''

Similarly he lived through the stories of Clara and Milly, Mary and Ermengarde. He could not shut his own mind from hers, nor could he close the slit, though it was within his power to widen it. Like some foul medusa, or some pulpy carnivorous plant, her soul unfolded and clung to his, until it seemed almost that his was the prisoner.

''And there was Trudie. Trudie worshipped me. She was a big girl, slow and a little stupid. She had come from a farm. She used to spend hours on my clothes, I encouraged her in various ways, until everything about me became sacred to Trudie. She lived for my little signs of favor. In the end she would do anything for me, which was very amusing, because she was very easily embarrassed and never lost her painfully acute sense of shame.''

But now he was at the door of his house, and the unclean trickle of thoughts ceased. The slit narrowed to the tiniest watchful crack.

He shephereded Mrs. Gunnison's body to the door of Tansy's dressing room. He pointed at the bound form huddled on the blanket he had thrown across the floor. It lay as he had left, eyes closed, jaw lolling, breathing heavily. The sight seemed to add a second crushing pressure to his mind, pressing on it from below, through its eye-sockets.

''Take away what you have conjured into it,'' he heard himself command.

There was a pause. A black spider crawled off Tansy's skirt and scuttled across the blanket. Even as there came the thought, ''That is it,'' he lunged out and cracked it under his heel as it escaped onto the flooring. He was aware of a half-cloaked comment, ''Its soul sought the nearest body. Now faithful King will go on no more errands for me. No more will he animate human flesh or wood or stone. I will have to find another dog.''

"Return to it what you have taken," he commanded.

This time there was a longer pause. The slit closed entire-ly.

The bound figure stirred, as if seeking to roll over. The lips moved. The slack jaw tightened. Conscious only of the black weight against his mind, and of a sensory awareness so acute that he believed he could hear the very beating of the heart in Tansy's body, he stooped and cut the lashings, removed the carefully arranged paddings from wrists and ankles.

The head rolled restlessly from side to side. The lips seemed to be saying, "Norman. . . ." The eyelids flut-tered and he felt a shiver go over the body. And then, in one sudden glorious flood, like some flower blooming miracu-lously in an instant, expression surged into the face, the limp hands caught at his shoulders, and from the wide-open eyes a lucid, sane, fearless human soul peered up at him.

An instant later the repellant darkness that had been press-ing against his mind, lifted.

With one venomous, beaten glance, Mrs. Gunnison turned away. He could hear her footsteps trail off, the front door open. Then his arms were around Tansy, his mouth against hers.

CHAPTER XX

THE FRONT DOOR closed. As if that were a signal, Tansy pushed him away while her lips were still returning his kiss.

"We daren't be happy, Norman," she said. "We daren't be happy for one single moment."

A disturbed and apprehensive look clouded the longing in her eyes, as if she were looking at a great wall that shut out the sunlight. When she answered his bewildered question, it was almost in a whisper, as if even to mention the name might be dangerous.

"Mrs. Carr—"

Her hands tightened on his arms as though to convey to him the immediacy of danger.

"Norman, I'm frightened. I'm *terribly* frightened. For both of us. My soul has learned so much. Things are different from what I thought. They're much worse. And Mrs. Carr—"

Norman's mind felt suddenly foggy and tired. It seemed to him almost unendurable that his feeling of relief should be broken. The desire to pretend at least for a while that things were rational and ordinary had become an almost overwhelming hunger. He stared at Tansy groggily, as if she were a figure in an opium dream.

"You're safe," he told her with a kind of harshness in his voice. "I've fought for you. I've got you back, and I'm going to hold you. They can never touch you again, not one of them."

"Oh, Norman," she began, dropping her eyes, "I know how brave and clever you've been. I know the risks you've run, the sacrifices you've made for me—wrenching your whole life away from rationality in the bare space of a week, enduring the beastliness of that woman's naked thoughts. And you have beaten Evelyn Sawtelle and Mrs. Gunnison *fairly* and at their own game. But Mrs. Carr—" Her hands transmitted her trembling to him. "Oh, Norman, she only *let* you beat them. She wanted to give them a fright, and she preferred to let you do it for her. But now she'll take a hand herself."

"No, Tansy, no," he said with a dull insistence, but unable to summon up any argument to support his negative.

"You poor dear, you're tired," she said, becoming suddenly solicitous. "I'll fetch you a drink."

It seemed to him that he did nothing but rub his eyes and blink them, and shake his head, until she came back with the bottle.

"I want to change," she said, looking down at her torn and creased dress. "Then we must talk."

He downed a stiff drink, poured himself another. But there was no stimulation. They didn't seem to be getting rid of his opium-dream mood, instead deepened it. After a while he got up and sluggishly made his way to the bedroom.

Tansy had put on a white wool dress, one which he had always liked very much, but which she had not worn for some time. He remembered she had told him that it had shrunk and become too small for her. But now he sensed that, in the joy of her return, she took a naive pride in her youthful body and wanted to show it to best advantage.

"It's like coming into a new house," she told him, with a

quick little smile that momentarily cut across her apprehensive look. "Or rather like coming home after you've been away for a long time. You're very happy, but everything is a little strange. It takes you a while to get used to it."

Now that she mentioned it, he realized that there was a kind of uncertainty about her movements, gestures and expressions, like a person convalescent after a long sickness and just now able to get up and about.

She had combed out her hair so that it fell to her shoulders, and she was still in her bare feet, giving her a diminutive and girlish appearance that he found attractive even in his stupid-headed, nightmarish state of mind.

He had brought her a drink, but she merely sipped it and put it aside.

"No, Norman," she said, "we must talk. There is a great deal I have to tell you, and there may not be much time."

He looked around the bedroom. For a while his glance rested on the creamy door of Tansy's dressing-room. Then he nodded heavily and sat down on the bed. The opium-dream feeling was stronger than ever and Tansy's oddly brisk voice and brittle manner seemed part of it.

"Back of everything is Mrs. Carr," she began. "It was she who brought Mrs. Gunnison and Evelyn Sawtelle together, and that one act speaks volumes. Women are invariably secret about their magic. They work alone. A little knowledge is passed from the elder to the younger ones, especially from mother to daughter, but even that is done grudgingly and with suspicion. This is the only case Mrs. Gunnison knew of—I learned most of this from watching her soul—in which three women actually cooperated. It is an event of revolutionary importance, betokening heaven knows what for the future. Even now, I have only an inkling of Mrs. Carr's ambitions, but they involve vast augmentations of her present powers. For almost three quarters of a century she had been weaving her plans."

Norman torpidly absorbed these grotesque statements. He took a swallow of his second drink.

"She seems an innocent and rather foolish old lady, strait-laced yet ineffectual, girlish but prudish," she continued. Norman started for he fancied he caught in her voice a note of secret glee. It was so jarringly incongruous that he decided it must be his imagination. When she resumed, it was gone. "But that's only part of a disguise, along with her sweet voice and jolly manners. She's the cleverest actress imaginable. Underneath she's hard as nails—cold where Mrs. Gunnison would be hot, ascetic where Mrs. Gunnison would be a slave to appetites. But she has her own deeply hidden hungers, nevertheless. She is a great admirer of Puritan Massachusetts. Sometimes I have the queerest feeling that she is planning by some unimaginable means, to re-establish that witch-ridden, so-called theocratic community in this present day and age.

"She rules the other two by fear. In a way they are little more than her apprentices. You know something of Mrs. Gunnison, so you will understand what it means when I say that I have seen Mrs. Gunnison's thoughts go weak with terror because she was afraid that she had slightly offended Mrs. Carr."

Norman finished his drink. His mind was slipping away from this new menace, instead of grasping it firmly. He must whip himself awake, he told himself unwillingly. Tansy pushed her drink over toward him.

"And Mrs. Gunnison's fear is justified, for Mrs. Carr has powers so deadly that she has never had to use them except as a threat. Her eyes are the worst. Those thick glasses of hers—she possesses that most feared of supernatural weapons, against which half the protective charms in recorded magic are intended. That weapon whose name is so well known throughout the whole world that it has become the laughing-stock of skeptics. The evil eye. With it, she can blight and wither. With it, she can seize control of another's soul at a single glance.

"So far she has held back, because she wanted the other two punished for certain trifling disobediences, and put into a position where they would have to beg her help. But now she will act quickly. She recognizes in you and your work a danger to herself.'' Tansy's voice had become so breathlessly rapid that Norman realized she must be talking against time. ''Besides that, she has another motive buried in the darkness of her mind. I hardly dare mention it, but sometimes I have caught her studying my every movement and expression with the strangest avidity—''

Suddenly she broke off and her face went white.

''I can feel her now. . . . I can feel her seeking me out . . . . She is breaking through—No!'' Tansy screamed. ''No, you can't make me do it! . . . *I won't!* . . .*I won't!*'' Before he knew it, she was on her knees, clinging to him, clutching at his hands. ''Don't let her *touch* me, Norman,'' she was babbling like a terrified child. ''Don't let her come *near* me.''

''I won't,'' he said sharply, suddenly stung awake.

''Oh . . . but you can't stop her. . . . She's coming *here,* she says, in her own body, that's how much she's afraid of you! She's going to take my soul away again. I can't tell you what she wants. It's too repulsive.''

He gripped her shoulders. ''You must tell me,'' he said. ''What is it?''

Slowly she lifted up her white, frightened face, until her eyes were looking into his. And she never once looked away as she whispered. ''You know how Mrs. Carr loves youth, Norman. You know her ridiculous youthful manner. You know how she always wants to have young people around her, how she feeds on their feelings and innocence and enthusiasms. Norman, hunger for youth has been Mrs. Carr's ruling passion for decades. She's fought off age and death for a long time, longer than you think, she's nearer ninety than seventy, but they're relentlessly closing in. It isn't so much that she's afraid of death, but she'd do anything, anything, Norman, to have a young body.

''Don't you see, Norman? The others wanted my soul, but she wants my body. Haven't you ever noticed the way she

looks at you, Norman? She desires you, Norman, that foul
old woman desires you, and she wants to love you in my
body. She wants to possess my body and to leave my soul
trapped in that withered old walking-stick body of hers, leave
my soul to die in her *filthy* flesh. And she's coming here *now*
to do it, she's coming here *now*."

He stared in dull horror at her terrified, unwinking, almost
hypnotic eyes.

"You must *stop* her, Norman, you must stop her in the
only way she can be stopped." And without taking her eyes
off his, Tansy rose and backed out of the room.

And perhaps there was something truly hypnotic about her
eyes, some queer effect of her own terror, for it seemed to
Norman that she had no sooner left the room than she was
back at his side, pressing something very angular and cold
into his hand.

"You must be very *quick,*" she was saying. "If you
hesitate for the tiniest *instant,* if you give her the slightest
opportunity to fix you with her eyes, you'll be lost—and I'll
be lost forever. You know the cobra that spits venom at its
victim's eyes—it's like that. Get ready, Norman. She's very
close."

There were hurried steps on the walk outside. He heard the
front door open. Suddenly Tansy pushed her body against his
so that he felt her breasts. Her moist lips felt for his own.
Almost brutally he returned her kiss. She whispered into his
lips, "Only be quick, darling." Then she slipped away.

There were steps in the hall. Norman lifted the gun. He
realized that it was unnaturally dark in the bedroom—Tansy
had pulled the shades. The bedroom door was pushed inward. A thin form in gray silk was silhouetted against the
light from the hall. Beyond the sight of the gun he saw the
faded face, the thick glasses. His finger tightened on the
trigger.

The silver-haired head gave a little shake.

"Quick, Norman, *quick!*" The voice from behind him
rose nervously.

The gray figure in the doorway did not move. The gun wavered, then swung suddenly around until it pointed at the figure beside him.

"Norman!"

CHAPTER XXI

SMALL RESTLESS BREEZES stirred the leaves of the oak standing like some burly guard beside the narrow house of the Carrs. Through the overlapping darkness gleamed the white of the walls—such a spotless, pristine white that neighbors laughingly vowed the old lady herself came out after everyone had gone to sleep and washed them down with a long-handled mop. Everywhere was the impression of neatly tended, wholesome old age. It even had an odor—like some old chest in which a clipper captain had brought back elegant spices from his voyages in the China Trade.

The house faced the campus. The girls could see it, going to classes, and it called to their minds afternoons they had spent there, sitting in straight-backed chairs, all on their best behavior, while a wood fire burned merrily on the shining brass andirons in the white fireplace. Mrs. Carr was such a strait-laced innocent old dear! But her innocence was all to the good—it was no trouble at all to pull the wool over her eyes. And she did tell the quaintest stories with the most screamingly funny, completely unconscious points. And she did serve the nicest gingerbread with her cinnamon tea.

A light came on in the hall, casting a barred pattern through the fanlight onto the old wooden scrollwork of the porch. The six-paneled white door below the fanlight opened.

"I'm going, Flora," Professor Carr called. "Your bridge partners are a bit tardy, aren't they?"

"They'll be here soon." The silvery voice floated down the hall. "Good-by, Linthicum."

Professor Carr closed the door. Too bad he had to miss the bridge. But the paper young Rayford was going to read on the Theory of Primes would undoubtedly be interesting, and one couldn't have everything. His footsteps sounded on the pebbly walk with its edging of tiny white flowers, like old lace. Then they reached the concrete and slowly died away.

Somewhere at the rear of the house a car drew up. There was the sound of something being lifted; then heavy, plodding footsteps. A door at the back of the house opened, and for a moment against the oblong of light a man could be seen carrying slung over his shoulder a limp and bulky bundle that might have been a muffled-up woman, except that such mysterious and suspicious goings-on were unthinkable at the Carrs', as any neighbor would have assured you. Then that door closed, too, and for a while longer there was silence, while the breezes played with the oak leaves.

With thriftless waste of rubber a black Studebaker jerked to a stop in front. Mrs. Gunnison stepped out.

"Hurry up, Evelyn," she said. "You've made us late again. You know she hates that."

"I'm coming as fast as I can," replied her companion plaintively.

As soon as the six-paneled door swung open, the faded spicy odor became more apparent.

"You're late, dears," came the silvery, laughing voice. "But I'll forgive you this once, because I've a surprise for you. Come with me."

They followed the frail figure in faintly hissing silk into the living room. Just beyond the bridge table, with its embroidered cover and two cut-glass dishes of sweets, stood Norman Saylor. In the mingled lamplight and firelight, his face was expressionless.

"Since Tansy is unable to come," said Mrs. Carr, "he's agreed to make a fourth. Isn't that a nice surprise? And isn't it very nice of Professor Saylor?"

Mrs. Gunnison seemed to be gathering her courage. "I'm not altogether sure that I like the arrangement," she said finally.

"Since when did it matter whether you liked something or not?" came the sharp answer. Mrs. Carr was standing very straight. "Sit down, all of you!"

When they had taken their places around the bridge table, Mrs. Carr ran through a deck, flipping out certain cards. When she spoke, her voice was as sweet and silvery as ever.

"Here are you two, my dear," she said placing the queens of diamonds and clubs side by side. "And here is Professor Saylor." She added the king of hearts to the group. "And here am I." She placed the queen of spades so that it overlapped all three. "Off here to the side is the queen of hearts— Tansy Saylor. Now what I intend to do is this." She moved the queen of hearts so that it covered the queen of spades. "You don't understand? Well, it isn't what it looks like and neither of you is especially bright. You'll understand in a moment. Professor Saylor and I have just had ever so interesting a talk," she went on. "All about his work. Haven't we, Professor Saylor?" He nodded. "He's made some of the most fascinating discoveries. It seems there are laws governing the things that we women have been puttering with. Men are so clever in some ways, don't you think?

"He's been good enough to tell all those laws to me. You'd never dream how much easier and safer it makes everything—and more efficient. Efficiency is so very important these days. Why, already Professor Saylor has made something for me—I won't tell you what it is, but there's one for each of you and one for someone else. They aren't presents, because I'll keep them all. And if one of you should do something naughty, they'll make it ever so easy for me to whisk part of you away—you know what part.

"And now something is going to happen that will enable Professor Saylor and me to work together very closely in the future—how closely you could never imagine. You're to help. That's why you're here. Open the dining-room door, Norman."

It was an old-fashioned sliding door, gleaming white. Slowly he pushed it aside.

"There," said Mrs. Carr. "I'm full of surprises tonight."

The body was lashed to the chair. From over the gag, the eyes of Tansy Saylor glared at them with impotent hate.

Evelyn Sawtelle half rose, stifling a scream.

"You needn't get hysterics, Evelyn," said Mrs. Carr sharply. "It's got a soul in it now."

Evelyn Sawtelle sank back, lips trembling.

Mrs. Gunnison's face had grown pale, but she set her jaw firmly and put her elbows on the table. "I don't like it," she said. "It's too risky."

"I am able to take chances I wouldn't have taken a week ago, dear," Mrs. Carr said sweetly. "In this matter your aid and Evelyn's is essential to me. Of course, you're perfectly welcome not to help if you don't want to. Only I do hope you understand the consequences."

Mrs. Gunnison dropped her eyes. "All right," she said. "But let's be quick about it."

"I am a very old woman," began Mrs. Carr with tantalizing slowness, "and I am very fond of life. It has been a little dispiriting for me to think that mine is drawing to a close. And, for reasons I think you understand, I have something more to fear in death than most persons.

"But now it seems that I am once more going to experience all those things that an old woman looks upon as forever lost. The unusual circumstances of the last two weeks have helped a great deal in preparing the ground. Professor Saylor has helped too. And you, my dears, are going to help. You see, it's necessary to build a certain kind of tension, and only people with the right background can do that, and it takes at least four of them. Professor Saylor—he has such a brilliant mind!—tells me that it's very much like building up electrical tension, so that a spark will be able to jump a gap. Only in this case the gap will be from where I am sitting to there''— and she pointed at the bound figure. ''And there will be two sparks. And then, when it's over, the queen of hearts will exactly cover the queen of spades. Also, the queen of spades will exactly cover the queen of hearts. You see, tonight, dears, we're positively fourth-dimensional. But it's the things you can't see that are always the most important, don't you think?''

''You can't do it!'' said Mrs. Gunnison. ''You won't be able to keep the truth hidden!''

''You think not? On the contrary, I won't have to make an effort. Let me ask you what would happen if old Mrs. Carr claimed that she were young Tansy Saylor. I think you know very well what would happen to that dear, sweet, innocent old lady. There are times when the laws and beliefs of a skeptical society can be so very convenient.

''You can begin with the fire, Norman. I'll tell the others exactly what they are to do.''

He tossed a handful of powder on the fire. It flared up greenly, and a pungent, cloying aroma filled the room.

And then—who knows?—there may have been a stirring at the heart of the world and movement of soundless currents in the black void. Upon the dark side of the planet, a million women moved restlessly in their sleep, and a few woke trembling with unnamed fears. Upon the light side, a million more grew nervous, and unaccustomed daydreams chased unpleasantly through their minds; some made mistakes at their work and had to add again a column of figures, or attach a different wire to a different tube, or send a misdrilled piece of metal to salvage, or re-mix the baby's formula; a few found strange suspicion growing mushroomlike among their thoughts. And perhaps a certain ponderous point began to work closer and closer to the end of the massive surface supporting it, not unlike a top slowly wobbling toward the edge of a table, and certain creatures who were nearby saw what was happening and skittered away terrified through the darkness. Then, at the very edge, the weird top paused. The irregularity went out of its movement, and it rode steady and true once more. And perhaps one might say that the currents ceased to trouble the void, and that the Balance had been restored. . . .

Norman Saylor opened the windows at top and bottom so the breeze might fan out the remnants of pungent vapor. Then he cut the lashings of the bound figure and loosened the gag from its mouth. In a little while she rose, and without a word they started from the room.

All this while, none of the others had spoken. The figure in the gray silk dress sat with head bowed, shoulders hunched, frail hands dropped limply at her side.

In the doorway the woman whom Norman Saylor had loosed turned back.

"I have only one more thing to say to you. All that I told you earlier this evening was completely true, with one exception—"

Mrs. Gunnison looked up. Evelyn Sawtelle half turned in her chair. The third did not move.

"The soul of Mrs. Carr was not transferred to the body of Tansy Saylor this evening. That happened much earlier—when Mrs. Carr stole Tansy Saylor's soul from Mrs. Gunnison and then occupied Tansy Saylor's bound and empty-brained body, leaving the captive soul of Tansy Saylor trapped in her own aged body—and doomed to be murdered by her own husband in accord with Mrs. Carr's plan. For Mrs. Carr knew that Tansy Saylor would have only one panic-stricken thought—to run home to her husband. And Mrs. Carr was very sure that she could persuade Norman Saylor to kill the body housing the soul of his wife, under the impression that he was killing Mrs. Carr. And that would have been the end of Tansy Saylor's soul.

"You knew, Mrs. Gunnison, that Mrs. Carr had taken

Tansy Saylor's soul from you, just as you had taken it from Evelyn Sawtelle, and for similar reasons. But you dared not reveal that fact to Norman Saylor because you would have lost your one bargaining point. This evening you half suspected that something was different from what it seemed, but you did not dare make a stand.

"And now as a result of what we have done this evening with your help, the soul of Mrs. Carr is once more in the body of Mrs. Carr, and the soul of Tansy Saylor is in the body of Tansy Saylor. My body. Good night, Evelyn. Good night, Hulda. Good night, Flora, dear."

The six-paneled door closed behind them. The pebbly path crunched under their feet.

"How did you know?" was Tansy's first question. "When I stood there in the doorway, blinking through those awful spectacles, gasping after the way I'd hurried with only the blind thought of finding you—how did you know?"

"Partly," he said reflectively, "because she gave herself away toward the end. She began to emphasize words in that exaggerated way of hers. But that wouldn't have been enough in itself. She was too good an actress. She must have been studying your mannerisms for years. And after seeing how well you played her part tonight, with hardly any preparation, I wonder I ever did see through her."

"Then how did you?"

"It was partly the way you hurried up the walk—it didn't sound like Mrs Carr. And partly something about the way you held yourself. But mainly it was that headshake you gave—that quick, triple headshake. I couldn't fail to recognize it. After that, I realized all the other things."

"Do you think," said Tansy softly, "that after this you'll ever begin to wonder if I am really I?"

"I suppose I will," he said seriously. "But I'll always be able to conquer my doubts."

There were footsteps, then a friendly greeting from the shadows ahead.

"Hello, you two," called Mr. Gunnison. "Bridge game

over? I thought I'd walk back with Linthicum and then drive home with Hulda. Say, Norman, Pollard dropped in to speak to me after the paper had been read. He's had a sudden change of heart on that matter we were talking about. On his advice the trustees have cancelled their meeting."

"It was a very interesting paper," Mr. Carr informed them, "and I had the satisfaction of asking the speaker a very tricky question. Which I am happy to say he answered excellently, after I'd cleared up a couple of minor points. But I'm sorry I missed the bridge. Oh, well, I don't suppose I'll ever notice any difference."

"And the funny thing," Tansy told Norman after they had walked on, "is that he really *won't*." And she laughed, the intoxicating, mischievous laugh of utter relief.

"Oh, my darling," she said, "do you honestly believe all this, or are you once more just pretending to believe for my sake? Do you believe that tonight you rescued your wife's soul from another woman's body? Or has your scientific mind already explained to you that you've been spending the last week pretending to believe in witchcraft to cure your wife and three other psychotic old ladies of the delusion of being each other and heavy knows what else?"

"I don't know," said Norman softly and as seriously as before. "I don't really know."

FAFHRD AND THE
GRAY MOUSER
SAGA

☐ 79176	**SWORDS AND DEVILTRY**	**$2.25**
☐ 79156	**SWORDS AGAINST DEATH**	**$2.25**
☐ 79185	**SWORDS IN THE MIST**	**$2.25**
☐ 79165	**SWORDS AGAINST WIZARDRY**	**$2.25**
☐ 79223	**THE SWORDS OF LANKHMAR**	**$1.95**
☐ 79169	**SWORDS AND ICE MAGIC**	**$2.25**

FRED SABERHAGEN

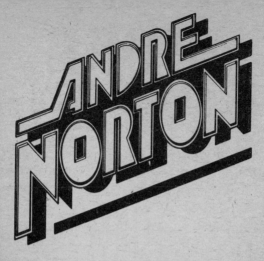

Classic stories by America's most distinguished and successful author of science fiction and fantasy.

☐ 12314	**CROSSROADS OF TIME**	$1.95
☐ 33704	**HIGH SORCERY**	$1.95
☐ 37292	**IRON CAGE**	$2.25
☐ 45001	**KNAVE OF DREAMS**	$1.95
☐ 47441	**LAVENDER GREEN MAGIC**	$1.95
☐ 43675	**KEY OUT OF TIME**	$2.25
☐ 67556	**POSTMARKED THE STARS**	$1.25
☐ 69684	**QUEST CROSSTIME**	$2.50
☐ 71100	**RED HART MAGIC**	$1.95
☐ 78015	**STAR BORN**	$1.95

ANDRE NORTON

"Nobody can top Miss Norton when it comes to swashbuckling science fiction adventure stories." —*St. Louis Globe-Democrat*

MORE TRADE SCIENCE FICTION

Ace Books is proud to publish these latest works by major SF authors in deluxe large format collectors' editions. Many are illustrated by top artists such as Alicia Austin, Esteban Maroto and Fernando.

Robert A. Heinlein	**Expanded Universe**	21883	$8.95
Frederik Pohl	**Science Fiction: Studies in Film** (illustrated)	75437	$6.95
Frank Herbert	**Direct Descent** (illustrated)	14897	$6.95
Harry G. Stine	**The Space Enterprise** (illustrated)	77742	$6.95
Ursula K. LeGuin and Virginia Kidd	**Interfaces**	37092	$5.95
Marion Zimmer Bradley	**Survey Ship** (illustrated)	79110	$6.95
Hal Clement	**The Nitrogen Fix**	58116	$6.95
Andre Norton	**Voorloper**	86609	$6.95
Orson Scott Card	**Dragons of Light** (illustrated)	16660	$7.95

Gordon R. Dickson

Fred Saberhagen

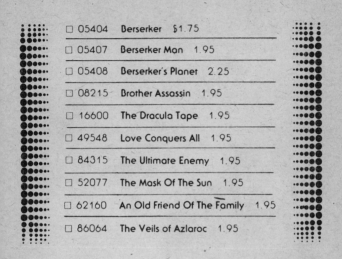

POUL ANDERSON